Before we step up the stairs of the bus, Maddie and I turn toward my — our — parents. The four of us fall into an emotional group hug. When we straighten, tears are running down my mom's face. "The War will end, and when it does, you girls will come home," she says, but I can't tell if she's trying to reassure us or convince herself that it's true. The War has been going on for years. It doesn't seem like it's ever going to end.

But I smile at my mom and nod. "I love you," I tell her and Dad.

"We'll take care of each other," Maddie says.

Then she and I take a deep breath and climb onto the bus.

TOMORROW GIRLS

Behind the Gates

Run for Cover

With the Enemy

Set Me Free

TOMORROW GIRLS

GIRLS

Behind the Gates

EVA GRAY

SCHOLASTIC INC.

New York   Toronto   London   Auckland
Sydney   Mexico City   New Delhi   Hong Kong

No part of this publication may be reproduced, stored in a retrieval system, or transmitted in any form or by any means, electronic, mechanical, photocopying, recording, or otherwise, without written permission of the publisher. For information regarding permission, write to: Scholastic Inc., Attention: Permissions Department, 557 Broadway, New York, NY 10012.

ISBN 978-0-545-31701-6

Copyright © 2011 by Suzanne Weyn.
All rights reserved. Published by Scholastic Inc.
SCHOLASTIC and associated logos are trademarks and/or registered trademarks of Scholastic Inc.

12 11 10 9 8 7 6 5 4 3   11 12 13 14 15 16/0

Printed in the U.S.A.   40
First printing, May 2011

Designed by Yaffa Jaskoll

TOMORROW GIRLS

Behind the Gates

Chapter 1

*O*kay, this is weird. I mean, it's not like we didn't know it was coming. But now that the moment has finally arrived ... I'm not sure I like it. Of course, I'm excited. But I'm also really scared to be leaving home for such a long time. We don't even know how long it'll be.

Out here in the sprawling, underground parking lots of what was once the Randhurst Mall, a mass of girls and boys mill around near our parents. We're all under fifteen, of course — after freshman year you go to work, usually for the war effort.

We're waiting for further instructions to be announced over the speakers mounted on the walls. It's been almost twenty minutes since the last announcement telling us to wait to be directed to the correct bus.

Shifting anxiously from foot to foot, I knit my shoulder-length blond hair into a single braid to keep the heat off my neck. It's the third week in August and it's hot, hot, hot. I never understand why school starts when it's still summer and the heat makes it impossible to even think.

"Where's Madeleine?" Dad asks.

Glancing around the lot, I find Maddie, my best friend in the world, sitting with her long, slender legs crossed on the concrete floor. I can tell how she's feeling just by looking at her. Right now she's definitely freaking out. Maddie's back is against a cement support column and her brown hair is pulled back into a headband and bundled up into the high, messy knot she was known for last year, when we were in seventh grade. Lots of girls started wearing it the same way and calling it the Maddie Frye Frizzle Bun. It makes her look prim and wild, all at the same time.

Maddie's eyes are cutting in every direction, hyperalert.

"She's right there," I tell my dad.

My mom lets out a deep sigh as she coils her own blond hair around her index finger. "When I was a girl this was such a beautiful mall," she remembers sadly. "It used to be crowded all the time. People had money to shop. These parking lots were all open-air, not underground garages. Of course, that was back before . . . you know . . . before the War."

Before the War. Adults must use that phrase a zillion times a day. *Before the War* . . . you could breathe the air and drink the water. *Before the War* . . . you could buy a pair of jeans for less than $500.

Placing her right hand on the back of my shoulder, Mom comes close to me. She's got something in her hand, but I can't see what it is because she has her fingers wrapped around it.

"What is it, Mom?" I ask.

She opens her hand and reveals a gold locket on a chain. Delicate filigree designs are etched into its surface. When she clicks the locket open with her nail, two tiny photos are revealed, one of my dad and the other of her.

3

"Below these pictures of me and Dad are photos of Grandma and Grandpa," Mom says. "Grandma gave me this locket when I was around your age. Now I'm giving it to you."

Taking it from her palm, I turn it in my hand, admiring its beauty and delicate workmanship. "I love it," I say honestly, but then I hesitate. "Maybe you should keep it until I come home," I suggest. "It's too nice. I feel like I might lose it or break it."

Mom takes the locket from me and unclasps it. "Don't worry about that," she says as she drapes it across my collarbone and it hooks in behind my neck. "I want you to have it now because you're going away. If you ever feel lonely, take it out and remember you're not really alone. Dad and I will always be thinking of you. Grandma and Grandpa, too. You can look at our pictures and know that we love you."

I throw my arms around Mom and, for the first time, my happy excitement gives way to a nearly overwhelming feeling of not wanting to leave. I'm going to miss Mom and Dad so much! Up until now my going away hasn't seemed entirely real. But now it hits me hard. In a very short while I will be departing, leaving my parents for the first time ever!

Mom holds me tight. Her heart is beating fast. She takes a short, sharp breath before she speaks. "I'm going to miss you so much, sweetie," she says in an emotional voice. "But I know you'll have a great time."

"I'll miss you, too," I say. I'm afraid to talk anymore because I don't want to cry and I'm suddenly worried that I will.

All at once every speaker crackles to life, making me jump. I step away from Mom as I strain to hear the static-buzzed words filling the underground garage.

"Bus card numbers one to seventy-five heading to Buffalo Grove, report to section A."

Maddie is instantly at my side. "Louisa," she hisses. "I can't find my bus card."

"You stuck it in your back pocket. Remember?" I tell her. Maddie can be a little scattered, especially when she's nervous.

With a relieved expression she pulls out the card we

were sent in the mail only two weeks ago. "Number two hundred and ninety-eight," she reads.

"And I'm two ninety-seven," I remind her.

"I know," Maddie says. "If we weren't together, I don't know what I'd do."

Maddie is much more nervous than I am about this. I'm actually kind of looking forward to it. Going to Country Manor sounds like time traveling — back to the world the way Mom and Dad have told me it used to be.

When my parents were young, people had cars that used oil, which was so inexpensive you could drive anywhere. Even just to the store. Sometimes even farther, to a whole other state. My mom still has pictures her parents took on a road trip to California when she was my age. The ocean looks so blue.

Not that there are even a lot of places to go anymore. The Gulf Coast and a lot of the South is basically gone since the hurricanes of 2018. Everyone up north wants to go south, where it's warmer, and people down south want to go north, where the storms aren't as bad. Seems like they all got stuck here in the middle of the country. You can barely afford to live in Chicago anymore.

But I love my hometown. And I have it easy, compared to most — my parents are both doctors, and I've never really wanted for anything. Except maybe my freedom. I'm thirteen. I'm sick of having to check in with my parents every half hour, even if I'm just going around the block. And it's just getting worse — the storms, the War. Curfew for under-fifteens went up to seven thirty p.m. last month.

Maddie has seen more of the world than I have. Her parents haven't had the money to keep her as sheltered as I've been. Maddie's dad has been gone most of our lives — he's a soldier. Right now, no one knows where he is, exactly. She hasn't heard from him in a year and a half.

Her mom's in the military, too, and she got sent away six months ago. Maddie moved in with us when she had to leave.

Maddie stares down at her card, reading and rereading the words.

COUNTRY MANOR SCHOOL. STUDENT 298. MADELEINE BALLINGER.

"My name looks so weird," she whispers, bending toward my ear.

"I know," I whisper back. "But you have to try to get used to it. And don't forget."

"I won't." Maddie wrinkles the ends of her card back and forth. "I guess we're toward the end. It doesn't seem like there are more than about three hundred kids here. I wonder where we'll be sent." There are other schools in different places around the country. All of us who are standing here waiting won't be going to the same location. I wonder how they decided who goes where.

I keep my eyes on the girls heading to the buses in A section. CMS keeps the girls' and boys' schools separate.

"No boys," Maddie says with a sigh.

"I heard there's a boys' school next to ours," I assure her. "I'm sure they'll have dances and stuff."

"It won't be the same," Maddie insists wistfully.

It's not that Maddie and I are boy crazy or anything. We've both had our crushes, of course. Plus we have guy friends we like to pal around with. Neither of us has ever attended an all-girls school before.

Still, it sounds like CMS is really posh, with all the latest equipment and facilities. I've heard they even have a huge indoor swimming pool.

At my old school I was on the swim team, before they disbanded all the teams two years ago. I love swimming, but I haven't been in a pool for a while. Using fresh water for something like a pool is obviously not an option anymore.

I turn back and look at my parents, and it hits me all over again how much I'm going to miss them. As much as I want this new freedom, I'm not entirely sure I'm ready for it.

"I wish we were going to Buffalo Grove," Maddie whispers, watching the girls climb onto their bus. "At least that's close to Chicago. We could get home on weekends and stuff."

"It doesn't mean the bus is actually going to Buffalo Grove," I point out. "That's only what they're calling it. Nobody knows where the bus will really go."

Not even Mom and Dad get to know exactly where the school really is. It's for their own safety.

Like everything these days. Keeping us safe.

Maddie nods and chews her lower lip, and I squeeze her hand.

Mom faces me and smooths the little hairs at the top of my forehead. "Remember everything we've gone over," she counsels, her voice barely a whisper. "Madeleine is your twin. When were you both born?"

"May first," I answer.

"And why don't you look alike?" she prompts.

"We're fraternal twins, not identical." Mom, Dad, Maddie, and I have been over this a million times. It's our cover story.

CMS is crazy expensive. You get to go if your family can pay the tuition. Like my family can. Mom makes lots as a brain surgeon. Dad earns even more. He's head of surgery at his hospital.

This leads me to another reason I'm excited about living away from home.

Since my parents are so smart, they expect me to be a

genius, too. But I'm pretty sure — basically positive — that I'm no genius, not by a long shot.

All I really want to do is swim. In the old days, I could have trained for the Olympics, but there are no Olympics anymore.

The sensible thing would be for me to study medicine. It would be useful and would delight my parents. I should at least *want* to learn to be a doctor like them. But what I really want is to be free of those expectations, if only for a little while. Maybe someday biology will make sense to me. In the meantime, well . . . Country Manor is going to set me free from all that.

I look at Mom and sigh. We might look just alike, but that's where our resemblance ends. I wish I could be more like her, but I'm just not.

Maddie's still holding my hand. "I can't believe how good your parents are being to me," Maddie says as my mom turns away to talk to my dad.

"They love you," I say. They really do — which is why they figured out how to get Maddie her new ID as my twin sister. Mom and Dad had to switch Maddie's papers and ID bracelet because Country Manor doesn't let you pay for other people's kids, even your daughter's life-long BFF.

Getting Maddie's ID bracelet must have been the hardest part. The bracelets are permanently, electronically linked to our wrists from the time we leave the hospital. All bracelets are updated and made larger when you turn five, and then again when you're twelve. Dad found a guy in a very scary part of the city who used a kind of handheld device to blur out Maddie's old info and change her last name to Ballinger on the bracelet. I think he charged a lot of money for this.

So now we're sisters, just like we've always felt.

Mom comes back and wraps Maddie in a hug. "Try to relax. Everything will be just fine," she says softly. "I promise I'll get word to your mom somehow —"

"Shh," Dad cuts her off softly. "Better not to talk here."

Mom nods. She rubs Maddie's shoulders.

We wait as busload after busload pulls out of the exit. Finally we hear: "Numbers two twenty-five to three hundred, heading to Blumberg Woods, report to the blue bus parked in section Y."

"Blumberg Woods is nice and close," Mom remarks brightly.

Maddie and I exchange a look. We know and she knows it's not where we're really going. I suppose she's trying to keep things as cheery and normal as possible.

Our suitcases have been sent ahead, addressed only to COUNTRY MANOR SCHOOL/CENTRAL HEADQUARTERS. PO STATION 5611. No street. No city. No zip code. Just PO Station 5611.

Without suitcases to carry, all there is to do is walk toward the bus.

Mom's blue eyes are wet with tears. "I'll miss you girls so much. Once you get there, call or e-mail me."

We line up. A woman with short hair comes out of the bus. She is tall and broad-shouldered, dressed in a crisp, white camp-style shirt, khaki shorts, and white sneakers. She has a name tag: MRS. BREWSTER.

Mrs. Brewster clearly means business. "Have all cell phones and other electronic devices ready to deposit into the bin before entering the bus," she barks at us like a drill sergeant.

Maddie and I look at each other with sharp alarm. I grab my cell from my pocket. "They're not getting my cell!" I declare firmly. "What am I supposed to do on the bus ride?"

"I'm sure it's just for your own safety," Dad says calmly.

What a surprise.

"He's right, honey," Mom says. "And you girls will be too busy talking and meeting new friends on the bus, anyway."

Maddie and I share another look and try not to laugh. Like we're going to be playing get-to-know-you games or something. Like we're still in third grade!

We inch toward the front of the line. The smile on Maddie's face fades, and she looks at me with her eyes full of questions. We're not little kids anymore — but what's going to happen now?

I just shrug. When we reach the bin, I toss in my phone first, and then Maddie drops hers.

Before we step up the stairs of the bus, we both turn toward Mom and Dad. The four of us fall into an emotional group hug. When we straighten, tears are running down my mom's face. "The War will end, and when it does, you girls will come home," she says, but I can't tell if she's trying to reassure us or convince herself that it's true. The War has been going on for years. It doesn't seem like it's ever going to end.

But I smile at my mom and nod. "I love you," I tell her and Dad.

"We'll take care of each other," Maddie says.

Then she and I take a deep breath and climb onto the bus.

Chapter 2

I sit watching the scenery go by on the interstate. The abandoned strip malls we've been passing become farther and farther apart until I stop seeing any at all. After a while all that passes by are fields and forests, fields and forests, getting slightly greener as we drive.

There's no way we're heading to Blumberg Woods — if we were, we'd have already been there an hour ago.

So where are we headed?

North. That's all I know from reading the signs.

Maddie is sleeping in the aisle seat beside me. At home we sleep in side-by-side twin beds. Her gentle snoring sometimes bugs me at night. Now it's different, though. Her snoring is a comforting reminder of home.

I wonder if Maddie misses *her* home — her real home, that is. Until her parents were both called away, the Fryes lived in a tiny apartment in the city.

Maddie and I met in kindergarten and we've been friends ever since. It's exactly as if we really are sisters, so this lie we are telling isn't much of a stretch. Saying we're twins, even fraternal twins, is funny, though — our looks are so opposite. Maddie resembles both of her dark-haired, brown-eyed parents, while I'm really fair, like my mom.

A low hum of conversation fills the bus. I put down my e-reader and look at the other girls. Mrs. Brewster sits up front and hasn't turned around the whole trip, as far as I've seen. But everyone's been pretty quiet, reading or listening to music or talking to their seatmates. I think we're all starting to get hungry and restless, though.

There's a group near the front that all look like athletes and have clearly already bonded. They're a good-looking bunch, all clear skin and toned arms and legs. They chat and laugh together as though they've been friends for years. "No one can return my serve," says a tall girl. She holds up an arm with a giant, fancy watch on it. "But my wrist is totally ruined. I have to wrap it up every time."

"Whatever," scoffs an Asian girl with her black hair in a sleek ponytail. "I fell so hard on my arm playing field hockey this year that I broke it. I was in a cast for the rest of the season."

One of the girls sitting near the sporty set isn't so chatty, but from the look of her well-muscled arms, she seems to be an athletic type. Her gleaming straight black hair is tied back with a gold cord into a high ponytail. Something about her face — the straight nose, the set line of her mouth — makes her seem regal, yet aloof and unfriendly. I don't think she's someone I'll get along with.

When the girl turns to the other athletes, though, she has a natural authority that makes them quiet down to hear her. "That's nothing," she says calmly. I'm pretty sure I detect — though just barely — the clipped beat of a Latin accent. "I was tripped on the basketball court and slammed my head so hard I was in a coma for three days."

For a moment the little group is silent.

"Wow!" the tall one says, filled with awe. "What's it like to be in a coma?"

"Yeah, I've always wanted to know that," says another girl.

I can't hear what she tells them because everyone has huddled around her. I can't even see her anymore without standing up.

Turning back toward our part of the bus — the back half — I notice a pretty girl with dark skin. Her black eyes are intense and her delicate eyebrows V with concentration as she types furiously on a notebook.

What's so urgent? It's not like we have homework yet.

I'd love to go talk to her but a slim, pale girl with white-blond hair is sleeping heavily in the aisle seat. Her presence makes it impossible to plop myself down beside the writing girl. Instead, I nudge Maddie. "Are you awake?"

Maddie's eyelids flutter. "Wha . . . ?"

"Are you awake?" I repeat.

19

"Now I am," she gripes, rubbing her eyes. "What's going on?"

"I need somebody to talk to," I admit, grinning apologetically.

Maddie straightens and leans across me to see out the window. "Where are we?"

I shrug. "Two hours north, as far as I can tell."

"Not in Blumberg Woods?" she checks.

I shake my head.

"Too bad," Maddie says sleepily, slumping against the back of her seat, closing her eyes.

I jab her again and lower my voice to a whisper. "Look at that girl over there. What do you think she's writing?"

Maddie stretches around to see behind her seat. "I don't see anyone writing," she reports, turning back to me.

I hoist myself high enough to see across the aisle. The girl is now chatting animatedly with the girl who had been sleeping beside her. *Chatting* isn't really the word; she's doing all the talking and her seatmate is simply listening in wide-eyed astonishment.

What could she be saying to make the other girl look so shocked?

Now I'm really dying to know what's going on with her.

"I'm going to the bathroom," I tell Maddie. "Maybe on the way back I'll be able to hear what that girl is saying."

"What girl?" Maddie asks.

"The one who was writing," I say. "If I stop to talk to her, you come join me."

"Why? I want to go back to sleep. I was up all night worrying about today. I'm tired."

"You weren't up all night. You were snoring," I tell her.

"Just go say hello to her. You don't need me for that," Maddie insists.

"I'd feel more comfortable with you there," I argue.

"Just say hi," Maddie repeats, yawning.

I always feel a little shy before I get to know someone. After that, I'm not shy at all. But if Maddie wouldn't join me, I'd feel more comfortable having a *reason* to talk to this girl.

Maddie curls up in the seat, resting her head on her arm, closing her eyes again.

She's clearly determined to go back to sleep, so I squeeze around her and head for the bathroom at the back of the bus. As I pass by the two girls I can hear only the briefest snap of conversation.

"Are you sure about all this?" the pale-blond girl asks doubtfully.

"Not the details, of course," the writing girl replies knowingly, "but in general, yes. Absolutely sure."

When I get to the back of the bus, the bathroom door is locked. I didn't need it, anyway — I just wanted to get up. But now what?

Suddenly an idea occurs to me and I slip one of my daisy-shaped plastic earrings out of my ear. I wait for a minute and then head back up the aisle.

When I'm near the two girls again, I drop the plastic daisy. Pretending to be surprised, I raise my hand to my ear. "I think I just dropped my earring," I say with a mild gasp.

The two girls peer into the aisle. "There," the girl who had been writing says, pointing at my earring on the floor.

"Oh, thanks!" I cry, stooping to retrieve it. "I'm Louisa Ballinger," I say, standing back up.

"Evelyn Posner," the writing girl replies with a friendly smile.

"I'm Jordan," says the pale-blond girl. Jordan waves for me to come closer. I lean in to hear. She's not satisfied with my position until I am practically squeezed into the seat with the two of them.

Jordan whispers, "Evelyn thinks this is a trap."

"What?" I ask, wrinkling my forehead. "What kind of trap? Who would want to trap us? The Alliance?"

"I don't know. Maybe," Evelyn replies. "I'm sure this is some kind of conspiracy, though."

I can't help but laugh. "A conspiracy to do what?"

"That's what I intend to find out!" Evelyn states with equal parts suspicion and excitement. "I tried to tell my parents this is all a setup," she goes on, "and they wouldn't listen, as usual. But that's fine. Now I can do some deep undercover work, finally be part of the war effort, you know?"

I don't know what I'd been expecting, but it definitely hadn't been anything like this!

I notice Maddie peering around the side of her seat. Her expression is asking me: *What is going on?*

I reply with a small shrug. I haven't decided what I think of Evelyn yet. "You really think this is an Alliance plot or something?"

"And, like, Mrs. Brewster is an Alliance *agent*?" Jordan adds.

"She could be," Evelyn allows, obviously warming to the subject. "Or she may be an unwitting pawn. The Alliance could be tricking her, too."

"I vote for Alliance agent," Jordan says. "She scares me." I have to agree — Mrs. Brewster is kind of freaky.

24

"It has to be a plot. Why else would the locations be so secret?" Evelyn adds.

"Well," I counter, surprised to hear the same old words coming out of my mouth this time, "they're trying to keep us safe, aren't they?"

Evelyn sighs and shakes her head, seeming to pity my naïve viewpoint. "Believe what you want, but I'm going to be ready." As proof, she tips her open notebook my way, revealing what she'd been writing so feverishly.

Lines. Arrows. Boxes. Squiggles and letters. LNR64 with an arrow pointing up.

"What is it?" I ask in a whisper.

"Lansing North, Route Sixty-four," she explains. She leans closer and lowers her voice to a whisper I only barely hear. "It's a map. When everything goes down, I'm making sure I can find my way home. And, see, I have it locked with a password." Suddenly the screen reverts to a picture of a kitten in a basket.

I raise my eyebrows skeptically. "Do you really think you need to do that?"

"How can you be so trusting?" Evelyn asks.

"It's just . . . school! What makes you so suspicious?"

"Maybe I'll feel better when I get my cell phone back," Evelyn allows.

I think maybe she's just nervous. New school, new place — we're all just trying to get a grip on this.

But, still . . . I'll feel better when I have my cell phone again, too.

When I return to my seat, Maddie's eyes are still wide-open. "What did you find out?" she asks.

"Oh, it's nothing," I say. I tell her about Evelyn's crazy ideas.

"What if she's right?" Maddie asks quietly. "Or maybe they're just getting us out of the way because . . . I don't know, because something really bad is about to happen?"

I pat her hand and say, "Things are already pretty terrible, aren't they? They just want to keep us safe."

Chapter 3

I shift in my seat, trying to stretch out my back a little bit. We've been traveling for what feels like forever, and I'm starting to get bored.

Maddie writes on her notepad. I see her trying to check her ClickNet page, but she can't get online. A box of snacks gets passed back — dried fruit and soy bars. We were told to bring our own canteens of water for the ride. Even fancy boarding schools don't throw money away on bottled drinks.

Outside the bus window I see nothing but trees. I've never seen so many trees. "Where are we?" I ask Maddie.

Glancing up, she blinks at me, as though my voice

has just called her back from some faraway place. "I don't know," she says. "I haven't really been looking."

Peering over the top of my seat, I check to see if Evelyn is still keeping track. Her eyes are fixed on the passing scenery, though she's not writing anything down.

I don't seriously think there's any danger. I do like the idea of knowing where I am, however.

Evelyn looks up and sees me, then gets out of her seat and comes over. She leans in to us and whispers, "From what I can tell, we've been going northwest this whole time, so we're probably in Minnesota somewhere."

"Oh, okay," I say.

"I don't think taking us closer to Canada makes any sense," adds Evelyn.

I raise my eyebrows, silently asking the question, *Why?*

"You know, because the Alliance has most of Canada now," Evelyn explains, as though it should be obvious, as if everyone is keeping close track of the War.

"Oh, right," says Maddie, and her face darkens with worry.

Evelyn returns to her seat and I follow her across the aisle. I lean over to her and whisper, "Could you please stop freaking out my" — I almost say *my friend* — "sister? She's worried enough as it is."

Evelyn shrugs. "I think we should keep our eyes open," she says. "Even if we don't like what we see."

This is totally the opposite of the way I see things. Things are usually fine, and smarter people than me are working hard to make sure that everything turns out okay. Like my parents. Like Maddie's parents.

Back in my seat, I watch the passing trees for a while longer until my eyes feel heavy and I let them slowly slide shut.

The squeal of the bus's air brakes shakes me from a dreamless sleep. We've stopped in front of a huge, old-fashioned building. It is — just as its name says — a country manor, a massive stone building with ivy creeping down its sides.

"Wow," I say to Maddie as I rub sleep from my eyes.

"Seriously wow," Maddie agrees, staring at the building wide-eyed. "This place looks like the old summer house of a queen or something."

"I know." All my worries about CMS disappear. How cool is this, to be living in a palace?

Slowly we all rise from our seats, gathering the few things we brought on board. Maddie gets up and stretches. "Here we go."

A shiver of excitement shoots through me.

"Yeah, here we go," I say as we move into the aisle and let the flow of girls carry us along. We huddle together outside the bus, awaiting further instructions.

There's a big lake about fifty yards to the right of the school. It extends behind the building, so I can't actually tell how big it is. Off in the distance, on the other side of the water, an equally majestic building is bathed in a soft pinkish-amber glow.

Mrs. Brewster stands in front of the group and claps her hands for attention. "I am Mrs. Brewster, headmistress here at Country Manor School." She gestures toward another woman in shorts and a white T-shirt. She reminds me of a gym teacher we had last year. "This is Devi, assistant headmistress."

Devi nods her head curtly without smiling.

Evelyn, a few feet away from Maddie and me, throws up her hand and starts speaking at the same time. "When do we get our phones back?"

"You don't." Mrs. Brewster's voice is clipped.

A wave of outraged whispers spreads through the crowd of girls.

"You wouldn't be able to use them here, anyway," Mrs. Brewster insists. "There's not a radio tower for miles. Absolutely no reception. There's not even a TV at the school."

"All my phone numbers and addresses are stored in my phone," the girl who claimed to have been in a coma says. "I need to have it back so I can write letters."

Mrs. Brewster shakes her head. "There is no mail service in or out of Country Manor."

Now the swelling wave of grumbling protest is even louder. Mrs. Brewster claps again, sharply, and everyone quiets. "Must I remind you girls that the United States is at war? Your parents have paid their hard-earned money to send you to a safe place, away from the threats of the Alliance. Country Manor School has given your families our pledge to provide you with the finest education while ensuring your safety at all costs."

"That again. Our safety," Evelyn scoffs to the girl beside her, but loud enough that most of us hear. "Everything is for *our safety*."

"That's right, young lady, it is," Devi says.

"Your cell phones are of no use to you and may still be trackable by Alliance surveillance. For that reason they are being held in a different facility," Mrs. Brewster explains.

Evelyn turns to me. "If there's no radio tower, how could they pick up a signal?"

Mrs. Brewster's eyes dart toward her, disapproving. I stare straight ahead. It's clear to me that in less than ten minutes Evelyn Posner has managed to put herself on Mrs. Brewster's troublemaker list, and I don't want my name added just because we're standing near each other.

"Silence, everyone," Mrs. Brewster's voice booms.

"We have a lot to go over today, but first, please hand all your electronic devices to Emmanuelle."

Confused, we all turn and see a young Indian woman with black, chin-length hair coming toward us, carrying a big box. She looks a lot like Devi, and she's also dressed the same as the others, in khaki shorts and a cotton camp shirt. The only distinctive item she wears is a red silk neck scarf with an orange paisley design swirling through it.

"That means everything," shouts Mrs. Brewster. "Note-pads, cameras, computers, music players. If we find that you've held back anything, your punishment will be severe."

"What are they going to do, throw us in jail?" Evelyn scoffs, but more quietly. No one responds. We're all taking this very seriously. Something in Mrs. Brewster's manner tells us that she is not a woman to be messed with. I don't understand why Evelyn doesn't realize this.

Reluctantly, we all line up to drop what we have into the box Emmanuelle holds. "I haven't finished the book I was reading," Maddie complains when she reaches the front of the line. She clutches her reader.

"You can finish it some other time," Emmanuelle says.

"Does that mean we get our things back tomorrow?" Maddie asks.

"I did not say that," Emmanuelle replies. "In the box, please."

Evelyn is next. She takes an MP3 player from her bag and tosses it into the box.

"Is that everything?" Emmanuelle inquires.

"Uh-huh," Evelyn replies, looking away.

Emmanuelle's eyes narrow and she is clearly not convinced. "I'd like to look in your bag," she tells Evelyn.

"There's nothing electronic in there," Evelyn protests.

"Your bag," Emmanuelle insists sternly.

Evelyn huffs with annoyance. "I said —"

Emmanuelle takes Evelyn's bag and peers into it.

"That's very important. I need it!" Evelyn complains when Emmanuelle pulls out her notepad, the one with the maps and directions in it. "My notes on . . ." Evelyn's voice trails off.

"Notes on what?" Emmanuelle asks.

When she asks this question my throat goes dry. Why didn't Evelyn just hand over the notepad in the first place?

Evelyn hesitates before answering Emmanuelle's question.

I feel an impulse to step forward and help her — to offer a cover story, a believable explanation. But I think this will seem strange and I don't really have the nerve to do it. So I say nothing.

"I have personal notes on my feelings about leaving home and coming here to Country Manor," Evelyn finally says, in a cool, even tone. "As a half-Irish, half-African-American student I feel my experience here will be useful to other minority students of mixed race and maybe I'll write a magazine article about it . . . or something like that."

Emmanuelle eyes Evelyn coolly as she places the notepad in the box with the other electronics. "We'll take good care of it," she says.

Evelyn returns, looking dejected, and stands just behind Maddie and me. "I hope she doesn't look at my maps," she whispers.

"You're half-Irish?" Maddie inquires. "I'm a quarter Irish."

Evelyn raises her hand and offers a light fist bump that Maddie returns. "My mom is named Fiona Kelly," Evelyn says.

Finally, everything electronic is collected. But we're not done. Mrs. Brewster claps her hands sharply for our attention. "For your own protection we will be holding all jewelry and other valuables in these metal lockboxes. Please gather any personal effects and bring them forward."

All around me the girls start taking out their earrings and pulling off their bracelets and necklaces. After losing our phones and notepads and music, this doesn't feel like such a big deal. But I finger my locket nervously. I don't know what to do. I would like to keep it safe — but I don't want to part with it, not so soon.

I feel eyes burning into me. When I turn I see that Mrs. Brewster is looking directly at my locket.

Responding to the order implied in her stare, I reluctantly reach back to unclasp the locket's chain. My hand trembles slightly. I can't stand to part with this. It would be like giving away my parents — and my grandparents!

I hide the locket in my closed palm. Glancing at Mrs. Brewster, I'm happy to see that she's no longer focused on me. She's moved on to staring down other girls who are hesitant about removing items of jewelry.

With my gaze still on the headmistress, I put my hand in my shorts pocket, letting the locket fall into it. I hope they don't have any kind of metal detection device.

I approach and deposit my earrings and a silver bracelet I took from my pack. Fortunately no sirens or alarms blare as I walk away, my locket still hidden in my pocket.

But as I head back toward Maddie and Evelyn, a different noise makes me turn toward the building across the lake. A silver bus has pulled in front of it.

"I see you all gazing curiously at that building across the lake," Mrs. Brewster says.

"Is it the boys' school?" someone asks.

Mrs. Brewster clears her throat, unhappy about being interrupted. "Yes. And I advise you to forget it's there. It is off-limits to you. Completely off-limits. The way around the lake through the woods here is the natural habitat of the poisonous Mississauga rattler. Believe me, you don't want to get bitten with Mississauga venom. It kills instantly. And for you swimmers in the group, this lake is so polluted that should you jump in to swim across, you will be too sick to make the trip back."

Mrs. Brewster stares at me again when she says this. I don't know how to feel about it. I guess I'm flattered that she recognizes me as a swimmer. It must be something about my build, but it makes me feel strange just the same.

Evelyn Posner tilts her head. "For a polluted lake, it sure sparkles," she notes.

Once more, Mrs. Brewster casts a sour, annoyed glance at Evelyn, but makes no comment.

"Wait for your name to be called," Mrs. Brewster instructs us, "and be ready to present your ID bracelet."

This is not a strange request. We're all used to holding out our wrists all the time, like at school and security checkpoints and that kind of thing. They might as well be surgically attached to our bodies instead of just linked around our arms. We can't even get into most buildings without a bracelet check.

"Anne Abadi," Devi calls, reading from a clipboard. "Alice Abbott."

Anne Abadi is a girl with long dark hair and Alice Abbott is her opposite, fair with mousy brown hair. The girls step forward, raising their left hands.

I expect Devi to produce a scanner. But she doesn't.

Instead, she holds up thick black clippers.

I wonder what she plans to do with those. I've never seen anything like them.

Maddie and I exchange glances.

Our expressions change into horrified stares of disbelief as Devi raises Anne Abadi's wrist and the scissors. She looks like she's about to snip it off, but that can't be true. All our lives we've been told that nothing can remove an ID bracelet.

A gasp travels across the crowd of girls as a low, electric zap sound comes from the clippers. In the next second, Anne's bracelet is in Devi's hand.

Anne's eyes are wide. Her jaw drops in shock. We all understand how she feels. It's as though Devi removed one of her fingers.

I slap my right hand over my left wrist and clutch it to my chest. This can't be happening! Without my ID bracelet I won't be able to do anything, to go anywhere. Without my bracelet who will I be? I'm not even sure!

Maddie and I look at each other. What's going on? "Maybe . . . they'll scan them all together and return them later," Maddie suggests. "Or they need to keep them somewhere safe, like everything else?"

"Hmmm . . . maybe . . . I guess so," I murmur uncertainly. I watch as girl after girl has her bracelet cut off. It's obvious that each one is disturbed by this. The girls frown or chew their fingernails; some even well up with tears, sniffling and rubbing their pink noses as they return to the group empty-wristed.

"Jordan Baker." The pale blonde who was sitting beside Evelyn on the bus approaches Devi. Cringing, she presents her arm to Devi, but then pulls back. Jordan can't bring herself to do it. Devi grabs at Jordan's wrist and they start an awful sort of tug-of-war, Jordan struggling to pull away, Devi trying to hold the clippers with one hand and pry Jordan's wrist away from her body with the other.

"I *need* your *bracelet*, Ms. Baker," Devi commands.

Jordan shakes her head. "I can't."

"Yes, you can, Ms. Baker. It's for your own safety."

We're all staring at the showdown. Evelyn rolls her eyes when she hears the thing about our safety again, but everyone is too stunned to move.

With a sharp yank, Devi grabs Jordan's bracelet, abruptly snipping it off. The girl looks at her in shocked disbelief. Then Jordan bends forward and vomits onto the dirt.

"Some people are *way* too attached," the coma girl jeers loudly. The tall tennis-playing girl snickers at the taunt, but she is the only one. The rest of us can totally relate to how Jordan Baker is feeling.

Jordan stands up and sees Mrs. Brewster and Devi glaring at her. "Sorry," she mutters. "I must be, you know, carsick or something."

I actually feel a little nauseated myself. I don't think I've ever been in a car or a bus for as long as we just were. I've certainly never been carsick, but maybe this is what it feels like.

"Louisa Ballinger," Devi calls. As I step forward and

present my wrist, I feel a sharp kick of anxiety in the pit of my stomach, but try to conceal it by keeping my face expressionless.

My skin tingles as Devi inserts the bottom blade between my bracelet and my arm. I look away when the electric buzz runs up the blades of the scissors. With a click, my ID falls free and Devi catches it. Quickly, she tosses it into the metal box with the others.

I'm amazed at how emotional I feel. Tears collect in my eyes but I force them down. It's as though I've been set adrift in some strange new world where no one knows me and I have no way to identify myself. I'm frightened even though I know it's silly.

"Madeleine Ballinger."

I look to Maddie but she is absently gazing out over the lake.

"Madeleine Ballinger," Devi repeats more loudly.

I poke Maddie and she turns sharply toward me. "What did you do that for?" she asks.

"She's calling you."

Maddie blinks, not understanding my meaning.

Devi is almost shouting now. "Madeleine Ballinger, please come forward and present your identity bracelet."

"Oh!" Maddie cries with a start. "That's me!"

"Yeah, that's you," I say, gently nudging her forward.

Maddie rushes toward Devi, extending her arm. "Sorry! Sorry! I just didn't hear you," she apologizes.

"From now on, pay attention," Devi insists impatiently.

I rub my forehead and sigh. How will we ever pull off this twin thing if Maddie can't even remember that her last name is supposed to be Ballinger and not Frye?

I'm surprised that Maddie doesn't seem to mind when Devi cuts off her bracelet. Is she relieved to be rid of her false identity? I think she is. Because I know her so well, I catch the glint of happiness that flashes in her eyes as Devi tosses the bogus bracelet into the metal box.

What's even more surprising to me, though, is that my feelings are hurt. I guess I'd assumed she'd be overjoyed to be twins. Hadn't we always been closer than sisters?

Stop! I tell myself. Maddie is no happier about this than the rest of us. She can't possibly be.

As Maddie walks back toward me, Evelyn raises her hand. Once more she doesn't wait to be called on before launching into the question everyone is dying to ask. "When will we get our bracelets back?"

"Ms. Posner, let's clear something up right now. Wait to be acknowledged before speaking," Mrs. Brewster scolds Evelyn. "This habit you have of speaking out whenever you feel the urge will not be tolerated here at Country Manor."

Evelyn's eyes widen; the reprimand has shocked her. "I only wanted to know," she repeats, holding her ground, refusing to apologize, "when our IDs will be returned to us."

"When you leave Country Manor," Mrs. Brewster replies evenly.

"Excuse me?" Evelyn says in disbelief.

"You don't need them here, and we don't want them to be lost or stolen. It's for your own protection."

Why wasn't I surprised to hear *that*?

"They don't come off," Evelyn argues. "They are permanently fastened to our wrists. They can't be lost or stolen."

"There are ways to do it," Mrs. Brewster replies. She gestures toward Devi, who holds up the electrical scissor-cutting device. "As you can plainly see."

"Teresa Balmer," Devi calls out, ending the debate between Evelyn and Mrs. Brewster.

"This isn't right," Evelyn grumbles.

"Don't worry about it," Maddie says comfortingly. "We really don't need them here. It's not like we'll be going anywhere."

"Speak for yourself," Evelyn says in a whisper.

Maddie gives Evelyn a reassuring hug and I cringe inwardly.

Still, as the cutting continues, I keep looking at my own bare wrist. I feel so strange without my bracelet — vulnerable or naked, somehow. I definitely don't feel safe or protected.

Chapter 4

"Louisa Ballinger, Madeleine Ballinger, Rosemary Chavez, and Evelyn Posner, step forward, please," Emmanuelle calls. She seems pleasant and her dark eyes are pretty. I feel more relaxed with her, maybe because she's one of the only teachers here who's smiled since we arrived.

We're in the residence hall, behind the main building. Even though the front of Country Manor looks royal, the back building is an entirely different story. It's plain and functional, no-frills. The windows have bars on them, which is a little creepy, but the views are lovely.

The four of us step forward and I take a quick, unhappy breath when I see the girl named Rosemary Chavez. She's the coma girl with the straight black hair and snooty attitude.

Rosemary Chavez raises her hand and Emmanuelle acknowledges her with a nod.

"I just want to say, no one calls me Rosemary. It's Rosie." She speaks to the group as though this is important information for everyone. This girl really thinks she's hot stuff.

Now that I know that Rosemary — Rosie — has a Hispanic last name, I look at her again. I can see it now. The girl has large dark eyes that go with her glistening hair. She's definitely Latina. I wonder where her parents come from. She doesn't really have an accent so I assume she's been raised in Chicago.

"You girls will be here in suite three-oh-two," Devi tells us.

"You mean the four of us will be living together?" Rosie Chavez asks. She gazes at Maddie, Evelyn, and me with unconcealed disappointment. We are obviously not the suite mates she had hoped for.

I don't exactly conceal my unhappiness about the situation. I'm not glaring at her or anything but I'm not smiling and waving, either.

My plan of avoiding her is pretty much blown. It's hard not to get to know someone you have to live with!

Emmanuelle unlocks a door and opens it, revealing a large main living room. Our bags are waiting in the middle of the floor, on a big rug. We step inside, following Emmanuelle, while the other girls are led down the hall by another CMS teacher.

The main room has a fireplace, a big table and chairs, and two not-terribly-ancient couches. Three doors lead off this space: a bathroom and two bedrooms, each with two desks and a set of bunk beds.

"I suppose you guys want to room together," Rosie sniffs at me and Maddie, as if being sisters is a weakness of some kind.

"Or maybe you two should split up," Emmanuelle suggests to Maddie and me.

48

"Why?!" we both ask at the same time.

Emmanuelle smiles, amused by our panicked outburst. "I know twins are close, but that's all the more reason to get to know someone else."

At the exact same moment, both Maddie and I glance at Rosie. We don't mean to. It just happens.

Rosie ignores us, though. "Are there any single rooms?" she asks Emmanuelle. "I'm sure if you contacted my parents, they'd be willing to pay extra for it."

"I'm afraid not," Emmanuelle answers. "Besides, you don't want to be alone, Rosie. That's no fun."

"I didn't think we were here to have fun," Rosie replies.

I *really* do not want to get stuck with her.

"Maddie snores," I offer.

"Not every night," Maddie protests, stung.

"True. True," I admit. "But what I'm saying is that I'm used to it. It doesn't even bother me anymore. In fact . . . to tell the truth . . . I snore, too. It's a twin thing. We share the snore gene, I guess."

"In that case, I guess it's you and me, bunking together," Evelyn says to Rosie with a friendly smile.

Rosie just looks at Evelyn and says, "I get the top bunk."

"Yeah, no problem," Evelyn replies, clearly annoyed by Rosie's bossy attitude. "It's your special day," she adds sarcastically.

I can't hide a snort of laughter and Rosie shoots me a dirty look.

Rosie pulls Emmanuelle to the side of the room for a quiet discussion. I guess she's still angling for the private room. That would be fine with me!

While they talk, I glance around the suite. I'm shocked to see that there aren't any computers anywhere. On closer inspection I notice that the electrical outlets are all plugged up. There are a few lamps and an overhead fan, but that's it.

I tap Maddie and whisper, "No computers. And look at the outlets."

"Oh, I guess that's why they took all our devices," Maddie says. "They probably can't get much electricity out here."

"I thought of that," Evelyn pipes up. "But this is a big campus — it should have its own power plant."

Emmanuelle has turned away from Rosie and is smiling at us. "Keys!" she announces brightly, handing us each an old-fashioned metal door key. I've never used one before, and my suite mates look just as dubious as I feel.

Rosie stares at her key for a minute, then rolls her eyes and stomps off into one of the bedrooms. Suddenly we hear a horrified shriek.

"What is THIS?" she shouts.

We turn and look into the bedroom doorway. We see that she's holding up a spiral-bound notebook — made of paper — and a pencil.

I plop onto one of the couches, a new wave of shock overtaking me. "Oh no," I say, barely able to breathe.

"They aren't honestly expecting us to *write*, are they?" Rosie demands.

Maddie runs to the other bedroom, and is quickly back with a report. "We have a whole stack of those, too," she tells me. "Do you remember any of our second-grade penmanship?"

I shake my head. I haven't actually written anything using a real pen and paper since then. How am I going to get through classes at CMS if we have to write?

"Don't worry," Emmanuelle says with a smile. "We will review penmanship with you. Now I'll leave you to settle into your new home."

"Will you be one of our teachers?" Maddie asks her.

"Yes. I teach nature skills."

"Does that count as a science?" I ask.

Emmanuelle nods. "That's right. You'll love it. It's very hands-on. The forest out there will be your lab."

"Where are we?" Evelyn asks.

Emmanuelle keeps her pleasant smile as she shakes her head. "Can't tell you that. It's for your —"

"Own safety," Evelyn finishes for her.

"That's right. Your safety is our most important concern here at Country Manor."

Emmanuelle looks us over and then claps her hands sharply, indicating that she's on to new business.

"I will come to get you at five o'clock to bring you to the dining hall, and after supper there will be some further orientation talks." With a wave, she heads out the door.

The minute Emmanuelle leaves, Evelyn plops into a chair and throws her arms wide. "Well, that was all very convincing, wasn't it?"

"What do you mean?" Maddie asks.

"They sent in the *nice* teacher to throw us off guard," Evelyn says. "If we had any suspicions about this place, Emmanuelle is meant to throw us off. Emmanuelle seems so nice and normal. She's young and pretty. Emmanuelle wouldn't trick us."

"But she *did* seem nice," I insist. "Why would that be a trick?"

"Look at us," Evelyn says, twirling her index finger in a circle. "Do you think it's an accident that the four of us are together?"

"Sort of," Rosie states. Then she mumbles, "A tragic accident."

Evelyn pays no attention to the insult. "The four of

53

us were the only ones who spoke up and asked any questions at all. We've been labeled, branded as troublemakers."

"I didn't make any trouble," I object.

"Oh, no?" Evelyn scoffs. "You were staring at that boys' school like you were ready to jump right in and freestyle it across the lake. Mrs. Brewster was talking to *you* when she said to not even think about it. Rosie wanted her stuff back and so did Maddie."

"And *you* bugged the entire staff, especially Mrs. Brewster," Rosie reminds Evelyn.

Evelyn stares levelly at Rosie. "I refuse to be pushed around or ignored, if that's what you mean," she replies with a dignified air.

"Yeah, something like that," Rosie snipes.

"So your point is . . . what?" I ask Evelyn.

"My point is that we're outlaws. We've been grouped together so they can keep an eye on us more easily," Evelyn explains.

"I am no outlaw," Rosie insists, folding her arms. "I am certainly not in the same category as you." She turns to me. "And I hope no one else saw that you didn't turn over your locket."

Without intending to, I gasp and clutch the locket in my shorts pocket. "I couldn't!" I blurt.

"Well, I should turn you in," Rosie says unpleasantly. "I don't want to be in trouble when you get caught with it. What you do reflects on the rest of us and I don't want to be associated with you if you intend to break the rules."

How obnoxious! I think.

Then I remember that I had the same thoughts earlier regarding Evelyn and feel a little ashamed of myself.

I take the locket from my pocket and hold it in my cupped palm. "I'll be really careful with it. I promise," I say calmly. "Just don't turn me in, please. It means so much to me. I'll leave it in my top drawer during the day and only wear it at night."

Rosie looks at me uncertainly but then softens. "All right. I won't tell. But you'd better not get caught."

"I won't," I say.

"I don't want to be thought of as a troublemaker," Rosie says.

"Like it or not — as far as the Country Manor staff is concerned — you already are," Evelyn says. "You've already dared speak truth to authority and that makes you dangerous."

"And everything you're saying makes you . . . nuts," Rosie counters. Evelyn's conspiracy theories are clearly deeply aggravating to Rosie — which makes me want to hear even more from Evelyn.

"Do you have any idea where we are?" I ask her.

"We're either in Chippewa County in Michigan or somewhere in northern Minnesota," Evelyn guesses. "At the end there the driver detoured off the highway and took that trail through the forest. The signs I could see were old ones from back when there used to be a Federal Parks Program. They were too faded to read."

"Thanks, Einstein," Rosie says. "I could have told you we're in some forest."

"But could you have told me that we're on the Canadian border?" Evelyn counters.

"How do you know that?" Maddie asks.

"We could have taken the Winter Road to the Northwest Angle leading into Manitoba. That's my guess because it's an unmanned port of entry into Canada. This could be the Provincial Forest all around us. I'm guessing we're still on the American side since we didn't stop for a border crossing."

Maddie and I and even Rosie stare at Evelyn, impressed. "How do you know all this?" I ask.

"Simple," she replies. "I knew something was up as soon as I heard about this place, so I tried to get prepared. I searched border crossings and I brought this."

Evelyn pulls a simple, old-fashioned compass from her jeans pocket. "When I realized we were going north, I was sure they'd head for Michigan because it's closer. But at a certain point we veered west instead of east."

Digging into her back pocket, she produces a very folded piece of paper. As she undoes the folds, a colored map, a computer printout, of the United States becomes visible. Smoothing it, she points to a spot near the

Canadian border at the top of Minnesota. "As best as I can figure, we're somewhere around here."

"That doesn't do us any good," Rosie insists sourly. "What does it matter where we are? We don't need to know that."

"You might want to know," Evelyn insists, "if you want to escape."

Chapter 5

I'm impressed by the dinner buffet — I have to stand there for a minute, staring at all the options. Pasta or salad or tofu burger or fried soycken or frozen soymilk . . . There isn't steak or anything crazy, but when we sit down, Maddie says her tofu burger is the best she's ever tasted. There's not a lot of it, though, just enough for one serving. Like always. (Mom says people used to count their calories because they were afraid of eating too *much*. I can't even imagine.)

The dining hall is huge, fitting in all three hundred of us at once. Apparently girls have been arriving by the busload all day, coming from Chicago and some other bigger cities in the area.

Girls are already sorting themselves into small cliques that sit together at the long tables. Evelyn, Maddie, and I eat together. Rosie joins the athletic crowd she befriended on the bus.

As I sit and eat a salad topped with grilled soycken, I continue to look around for electronics. I learn from some other girls also sitting at our table that the lack of outlets is just the beginning of the no-electronics story. CMS has no television, phone, or Internet service. Batteries are stockpiled but no one knows exactly where. At any rate, they're not telling us students where. Hydro- and solar-power sources fuel the lamps and water systems but everyone will need to get used to pens and pencils.

After we eat, we're told to assemble in another very big room right next door. Mrs. Brewster is there, sitting in a large, overstuffed chair. The rest of the staff surrounds her. Emmanuelle sits to the right of Mrs. Brewster, next to Devi. She smiles and waves to Maddie, Evelyn, and me as we enter.

When we're all settled on the carpet around the staff, Mrs. Brewster stands.

"I trust you all enjoyed your meal," she begins. She smiles and nods as a murmur of positive responses rises from the crowd. "We have some more school guidelines to go over now," she says. "Since this is the first day, we have gone later than usual. Starting tomorrow, evening curfew will be seven o'clock."

"Seven?!" Jordan Baker yelps.

"Let me remind you girls to *raise your hands* before speaking," Mrs. Brewster insists.

"Sorry," Jordan mutters.

"At seven you will be expected to be in your rooms. By eight, lights must be out," Mrs. Brewster continues. "Classes start at seven a.m., sharp, after breakfast, which is from five thirty to six thirty."

A girl raises her hand and Mrs. Brewster points to her. "Won't we have to get up in the dark?" she asks.

"Sometimes. Depending on the season," Mrs. Brewster confirms without a note of apology. "Every day we will have a lot to cover. That's why we rise early and go to sleep early. You girls represent the privileged children of the country, the inheritors of the earth."

61

"Who wants it?" a girl sitting in back scoffs. "They can keep it!"

I expect Mrs. Brewster to scold her, but she doesn't.

In bed by eight? Up by six? I haven't kept those hours since I was in the first grade. I don't know if I can even sleep at eight o'clock. Is it even dark at that hour? In the winter it will be, but not yet.

I'd been hoping for more freedom at Country Manor, but it's really strict. I'm not sure how I feel about all this.

"Whether you accept the challenges that lie ahead or not, they will assuredly fall to you," Mrs. Brewster says seriously. It's almost like she's been reading my mind. It actually scares me a little.

"Country Manor is not some luxury resort," Mrs. Brewster continues, freaking me out even further. It's as though she's responding to everything I've been thinking. "If that's what you are expecting, get rid of that notion right now. Every one of you will do her share. Kitchen duty, grounds patrol, and sanitation aide positions are assigned at the end of the week. Kitchen and sanitation jobs will rotate throughout the year, but patrol duties are an honor assigned only to girls who prove themselves deserving of a position in the Student League. Those posts will be held as long as the chosen girls prove themselves worthy and dependable."

"Big deal," Evelyn says under her breath. "You get to patrol the grounds. What an honor."

"All meals and classes will be taken here in the main building," Mrs. Brewster goes on. "Behind the main building is the gym, where the pool is located. Behind that is the athletic field. That field is where you girls will learn sharpshooting, archery, and survival skills. Pay close attention to these classes. What you learn will be applied soon, when you are sent on overnights in the woods."

I'm surprised to hear this — and from the looks on their faces, so is everyone else. Camping is not something anyone does anymore; it's not safe for a lot of reasons.

"Aren't there wild animals in the forest?" a girl asks after Mrs. Brewster points to her raised hand.

"And what about that rattlesnake you mentioned?" another girl blurts.

"If you pay strict attention during your classes, you will all be fully prepared before being sent out," Mrs. Brewster assures them.

A dark-haired girl raises her hand and is called on. "Why do we have to practice all this nature stuff?" she asks. "Isn't nature kind of ruined, anyway? I mean, who even goes outside?"

"Country Manor is located in one of the last of nature's unspoiled strongholds. We feel it's important for you girls to know nature so that you can protect it and restore the planet. When the natural world recovers from the current crisis, you will possess skills that might other-wise have been lost."

"Do you really think nature can recover?" asks a girl with long, straight black hair. "I mean . . . in school they told us that the planet has been polluted beyond any chance of recovery."

"They're wrong," Mrs. Brewster says. There is a pas-sion in her voice I wouldn't have suspected she was capable of. "CMS feels strongly that you girls need these skills we will teach you to be productive members of the New Society."

Mrs. Brewster says *New Society* just like that, like it's capitalized — like it's something we all know about already. But I've never heard that term before. It sounds kind of exciting, I have to admit. Maybe being a swimmer will have a place in this New Society, if they're teaching us to clean up the lakes or whatever. And the sharpshooting, archery, and survival skills stuff sounds cool to me, too.

And they have a pool!

During my swim team days, I didn't care that much about winning. Sometimes I won. Most of the time I placed.

Now I feel the stirrings of something new inside me. I glance at the clique of top athletes sitting in the corner and imagine myself sitting among them. It could happen if I give it my best shot.

Like a flash of light, all at once, I realize that being a champion swimmer is something I've wanted all my life. It just never seemed even remotely possible.

But I'm wondering if it's possible here. As much as I love my parents and I know they love me, being a doctor was the only thing that was considered important. It didn't matter that it wasn't what I wanted. It might be superstrict here, but I think I'm going to really like it at Country Manor.

After Mrs. Brewster finishes answering questions, we're allowed to wander around the grounds. "I want to read while we still have some light," Maddie says as we leave the building. "Do you mind if I head back?"

"Sure, go on," I agree. "See you back at the room."

We've put our keys around our necks on chains and we wave them to each other with ironic smiles. It's nice to have something like this to hang on to, now that we don't have our IDs anymore.

I watch her go, then take off on my own. Of course, the first place I head for is the lake. As I watch the reflection of the sky darken in the water, I notice that the boys' school is pretty well lit, even before nightfall.

The flutter of excitement I'd felt before grows a little stronger. I can figure out a stupid pencil — I'd been taught how, after all. It has been a while, but whatever; everyone else is on the same page. Literally!

Before she finished her speech, Mrs. Brewster had said something about progress reports being sent to our parents, but this isn't home. Mom and Dad will no longer be able to see me stumble over my math homework every single day like when I was in Chicago.

Of course, it isn't complete freedom. Far from it. I still have a curfew, and I am still a kid. But look at this — I am all alone, practically in the woods.

Maybe I've found a New Society, after all.

Chapter 6

On the first day of school we scramble to find the classes on the schedules we've been given. My first class is English. The teacher, Sasha, doesn't even greet us. "Copy this into your notebooks, ladies" is all she says. Then she turns to the old-style blackboard and picks up a white stick of something I don't recognize. With rapid movements she covers the blackboard in notes, all written in an artful, curved script. My grandmother wrote like this, I recall. Otherwise almost everyone prints these days.

Glancing around the room, I notice that everyone is having a hard time taking notes without their laptops or notepads. I actually get hand cramps from writing with the pencil provided on my desk. And forget using an eraser! They don't even work!

My notebook winds up full of scratch-outs and scribbles. It's a complete mess and I hope no one will check it.

The rest of our morning is spent on other familiar subjects — social studies, algebra, and science.

"Don't you think it's weird that all the English and social studies books are from before 1980?" Evelyn points out as we walk to our next class.

"The school is old, and it's probably hard to get supplies," Maddie suggests. "You know how hard it is to get anything since the War started."

"She's right," I say. Mom and Dad told me that back in the day, there were huge stores that sold tons and tons of cheap stuff. Everything was affordable because it was all made in countries where people didn't have any rights and no one made enough money.

But honestly, I might not have even noticed the old textbooks if Evelyn hadn't pointed them out. I like my classes — a lot. The teachers seem pretty nice, so far.

They're all young women with various accents and nationalities — except for Mrs. Brewster, who doesn't have any kind of accent and doesn't teach any courses. She's just in charge.

We're supposed to call all the teachers by their first names, like Devi and Emmanuelle and Sasha. It's hard to get used to, especially since things are pretty formal here otherwise. But the only last name we use is Mrs. Brewster's — and no one knows her first name. Evelyn calls her "Bunny" as a joke sometimes.

In the afternoon we have speech and debate. After that we have Emmanuelle for outdoor survival skills. I know afternoons will be my favorite. I'm not sure which of these two classes I love the most.

In every class we're told that we are part of the New Society. It doesn't take me long to figure out that in the New Society we will be the privileged elite who will be expected to lead the masses when the War is over. Our teachers keep referring to us as the *future of the country.*

"That's kind of obnoxious, don't you think?" Maddie

says to me at dinner. "Why should we be the future of the country just because we can afford to go to this school? If you think about it, it's offensive."

I shrug — I kind of like the idea. It gives me a feeling of having a serious purpose. I'd never felt like that in school before. Mostly all of it had seemed unimportant. All I could think was, *Why do we even have to know this stuff?* At CMS, I don't feel that way.

"Of course it's offensive," Maddie insists, replying to my shrug. "If your parents hadn't paid for me to be here, my parents couldn't have afforded it."

My eyes dart around quickly, making sure no one is listening. "Shh," I warn.

Maddie lowers her voice. "Now I'm a 'future leader' because I'm here. If I couldn't afford to be here, who would I be? A big nobody?"

"But you *are* here," I remind her.

"That's not the point."

I know it's not the point, but this is a touchy subject and I want to get off it. "Well, I'm just happy we're here," I say. "And you should be, too."

71

Evelyn sits down at our table. "I have to ask you guys something about science," she says. "Don't you think it's odd that we'll be learning an awful lot about starting fires, building explosives, and making poisonous gases?"

"I had fun building that fire today," I say.

"Sure, it was fun," Evelyn admits, "but don't you think it's a little weird that tomorrow we're going to learn how to blow stuff up?"

I only shrug, again, because I think that's going to be really interesting, too. For the first time in my life I enjoy science class. Maybe it is a little strange, but then, what's normal anymore?

On the second day of outdoor skills Rosie and I are paired up. I'm not exactly thrilled about this. The first thing we do is review fire-building from the day before. While I'm off in the woods collecting branches for kindling, Rosie stays behind arranging the stones in a circle. *She leaves me to do all the work while she sits and plays with rocks*, I complain silently to myself. *Does she think I'm her servant?* But when I return, a bundle of

72

branches in both arms, Rosie already has the beginnings of a fire.

"How did you do that so fast?" I ask.

"I just grabbed some small twigs for tinder to get started," Rosie says, sitting back on her heels. "Nice timing. We need the larger kindling branches to keep this thing burning."

Did she just give me a compliment?

I set my bundle down and we both get to work building a tepee-shaped structure that quickly lights. "You got nice dry branches. Good job," Rosie says as we back away from the rising flames.

Was that *two* compliments?

After teaching us to douse the fires and scatter the ashes, Emmanuelle hands us each a .22-caliber lightweight rifle for target shooting. Once more, Rosie and I are paired up. We lie side by side on a dirt mound facing two stands with paper targets stapled into them.

Emmanuelle shows us the correct position for holding the rifle and how to sight the middle of the target. "Remember, girls, even though these are relatively small rifles, they're still going to kick up on you when they're fired. You have to be able to find just the right spot below the target to compensate for that kick. It will take some practice to get it right. If you don't figure that out, all your shots will go high and you won't hit the center."

Emmanuelle shouts the commands and we shoot. Then she takes down the targets. Just as she predicted, my shots from the first round are all completely outside the bull's-eye area. Rosie's bullet holes cluster just above it. She checks her paper target and then reaches for mine. For some reason, I let her take it.

"Aim just below the target," she advises.

"Then I'll miss," I argue. I wonder if she's just messing with me.

"No, you won't," she says confidently, returning the paper. "Just try it."

Emmanuelle calls for another round of firing. Despite my misgivings, I aim low, like Rosie suggested.

When Emmanuelle shows us our results after that round, mine are much better. I haven't hit the center, but all my shots are now much closer than before.

I notice Rosie smiling down at her paper and lean over to see her result. Bull's-eye! One of her shots made it dead center into the middle.

"Wow! Nice work," I say.

"Thanks," Rosie replies.

"You should hang that on our front door," I suggest. "No one, not even Mrs. Brewster, will want to mess with us then."

Rosie laughs. "No, I guess not."

"How'd you learn to shoot like that?" I ask.

Rosie gets to her feet. "Just beginner's luck," she says.

"Really?" I question doubtfully.

"Yeah."

At dinner that night Maddie asks me what was going on with Rosie at the rifle range. "Did I see you guys laughing about something?"

"Yeah, we were kind of having fun. You know, Rosie isn't so bad, at least not when she's in her element," I say. "And her element seems to be the outdoors. You should see how fast she can build a fire."

No sooner have the words left my mouth than Rosie walks by. "Rosie!" I call, waving her over to the table. "Come sit!"

But Rosie doesn't even look at us as she carries her tray to the elite sporty girls' table.

"I guess she's not in her element anymore," Maddie quips.

I'm baffled and confused. I thought Rosie and I were friends now. I can't believe she'd just blow us off like that. If nothing else, we are suite mates. She could have at least waved.

Evelyn slides into a seat across from Maddie and me. "I've decided that I'm applying to the Student League," she tells us.

"What?" Maddie asks.

"You know, the group that does grounds patrols, including patrols after lights-out."

"Wait a minute. Wasn't it you who made a face and said it sounded dumb when Mrs. Brewster mentioned that?" I recalled.

Evelyn smiles sheepishly. "I know, but . . ."

"What changed your mind?" Maddie asks.

Evelyn eagerly leans in closer to us, clearly excited about what she's going to say. "The League members get special night-vision masks and keys to the main hall."

"Cool," Maddie says, nodding. "Totally cool."

"Seriously," I agree.

"Don't you think this could be the best way to dig up dirt on CMS?" Evelyn adds.

I have to laugh a little as I shake my head. "I should have known that was your real reason!" All these conspiracy theories are starting to seem more than a little ridiculous, but Evelyn won't give up.

"Isn't it a good idea?" Evelyn presses.

"It sounds like the best way to get in deep trouble," I comment.

"No, it's not," Evelyn disagrees, brushing away the idea with a wave of her hand. "Why don't you guys apply with me?"

"Not me," I state. "I'm fine with kitchen duty. Cleanup crew doesn't sound like much fun, but maybe in the kitchen I can grab some extra food."

"Getting fat off stolen food also sounds like a good way to get in trouble," Evelyn argues.

I laugh. "The way they work us in this place, I could eat twice the food and still not get fat."

"How about you, Maddie?" Evelyn asks. "Why don't you apply?"

"I don't know," Maddie answers. "I'm not sure I'd like it."

"Don't do it," I say a little too forcefully. I look at her pointedly. The last thing we need is for Maddie to call attention to herself. We want her to stay as below the radar as possible.

"Let her make up her own mind," Evelyn scolds mildly. "What are you, the bossy twin?"

"Yeah," Maddie agrees. "I'll make up my own mind, Ms. Bossy Twin."

Chapter 7

When Evelyn comes into English class with us on Friday morning, a student from another class hands her a note telling her to report for a League interview. Barely able to contain her excitement, Evelyn practically skips out the door.

"What about you?" I ask Maddie.

"I decided not to apply," she reports.

"Good," I say.

"It wasn't because you told me to," Maddie insists quickly.

"I still think you did the right thing," I say.

Just as class is letting out, Evelyn returns, wearing a smug little grin.

"How did it go?" Maddie asks as Evelyn takes a seat in a just-vacated desk near ours.

"Awesome," she replies confidently. "I totally played the system. I told them everything they wanted to hear and they ate it up!"

"So you're not on the no-fly list anymore?" Maddie asks.

Evelyn shakes her head emphatically. "I told them I was asking so many questions when we first got here because I was nervous. But now I'm a total CMS fan. They are *so* going to take me."

Maddie and I laugh. "In that case, do you promise to let us try on your night-vision mask?" Maddie teases.

"No way!" Evelyn replies, laughing, too. "Apply for the League and get your own!"

At dinner the kitchen jobs are announced. Maddie gets cleanup, and she doesn't look happy about it. "Why do I have to pick up after all these rich kids?" she complains bitterly over her dinner of soycken wings and rehydrated string beans.

"Everyone will have to do it, eventually," I remind her as I shovel tofu chili into my mouth. "My assignment is kitchen staff. That's not any better."

"Of course it's better," Maddie says hotly. "It's much better! You'll be preparing food or putting it out on the buffet tables. I'll be picking up garbage."

"All these jobs rotate," I say, but Maddie doesn't want to hear it.

Evelyn brings over a bowl of pasta with tomato sauce and takes a seat.

"You know it's because of who I am," Maddie goes on, so wrapped up in her argument that she doesn't even stop to acknowledge Evelyn's presence. "If my parents were doctors, I bet I wouldn't have pulled cleanup duty. If my parents were rich and famous like —"

Alarm bells clang in my head. Evelyn is sitting down right next to us! And who knows what other girls could be quietly tuned in to our conversation?

"Your parents *are* my parents, silly," I say loudly. "Any way they treat me is the same way they are going to treat you . . . because we're a family!"

Maddie blinks. And then bites her lips as she realizes what she almost did. "Yes, I know," she mumbles. "I was just goofing around."

"You're such a weirdo sometimes," I say lightly. She really has to be more careful!

Maddie rises from her chair, gazes around the cafeteria, and then just leaves without another word.

Normally I would follow her out to make sure she's okay, but right now I just don't want to. Before coming to CMS, I never really realized how dramatic and negative Maddie is . . . about everything! Even Evelyn, with her crazy theories, at least tries to have fun and get along. Heck, even Rosie is fun during class!

"Hey, guess what?" Evelyn says brightly, breaking me out of my frustrated thoughts. "I'm in! I'm a Leaguer!"

She raises her hand high and I slap it in congratulations.

"I wanted to tell Maddie, too — what's bothering her?" Evelyn asks.

"Oh, it's nothing," I say dismissively. "She's just way too touchy sometimes."

"Is it because she's got kitchen duty? Everyone will have it eventually," Evelyn says. Then she grins. "Except League members, of course."

I roll my eyes but smile. "Of course. You guys are going to be *much* too busy being the upstanding junior citizens of the New Society."

Even if I wanted to go after Maddie, I can't leave right now. After dinner, at six thirty, the kitchen staff is going to show us where we need to be for the next two weeks.

"Hey, now that you're in the League, can we keep the lights on all night?" I ask playfully.

"No way," Evelyn says, suddenly serious. "I have to play by the rules or my cover will be blown."

On schedule, Mrs. Brewster appears and steps to the front of the room. "Those students assigned to kitchen staff for the next two weeks, please report to me for orientation. Those assigned to the cleanup crew, go see Devi."

Turning, I see Devi standing near the buffet table. Maddie is already off to a bad start, missing her training session.

As I start to get up, Evelyn puts her hand on my arm and leans closer. "Tell me *everything* you see in the kitchen," she whispers.

"Will do," I promise with a smile. "I'll report every suspicious tofu dog I see."

"Just keep your eyes open," Evelyn insists.

About twenty of us gather around Mrs. Brewster. She takes a folded piece of paper from her pocket and lays it flat on the nearest table. "Find your assigned shift here. This is the shift you will work for the entire two weeks of your kitchen staff rotation."

The girls crowd the table to see if they've gotten breakfast, lunch, or dinner. I hang back and notice that Rosie is over by Devi with the other cleanup crew girls. I wonder if she feels as insulted by the cleanup assignment as Maddie does. All different girls are in her group. It doesn't seem to me that anyone has been singled out to work cleanup for any reason. Why does Maddie have to be like that?

Once the first rush of girls leaves the table, I move forward to find my assignment. I groan when I see it.

Breakfast! And I have to be there for prep work by four thirty in the morning!

"Follow me to the kitchen," Mrs. Brewster instructs us. She leads us to a large room with a high ceiling. The fixtures and cabinets look about a hundred years old, deep white porcelain sinks, white metal cabinets. Bulky ovens with heavy doors. The walls are all covered in large white tile and the small floor tiles are in a black-and-white checkerboard pattern.

I'm surprised to find myself taking note of all these details — Evelyn telling me to keep my eyes open seems to have made me more observant.

Mrs. Brewster takes us around, showing where everything is located. In the refrigerator I see the usual — white lettuce, soy cheese, soy milk — and the pantries are full of canned vegetables and fruits. Most of the products are from NutriCorp, which has a big Canadian maple leaf on its logo. Food from a Canadian corporation. I smile to myself. Evelyn will definitely have a wild idea about that!

I'm back in the suite by seven, just in time for curfew.

Evelyn and Rosie's door is closed. The door to the room I share with Maddie is also shut tight.

It's just as well. Whatever's bugging Maddie, I'm not ready to listen to it. I'm just as happy not to see her. I would like some company, though.

I sigh, alone in the dark living room. The only light is the last rays of dusk making it through the tall windows. I'm just not in the mood to sleep right now and I wish Evelyn were still up.

I remember that last night we were given an oil lamp for our table. It's so that we can do a little homework at night in the winter months, but even these need to be doused by eight, when the last round of Student Leaguers checks in and we're expected to go to sleep. I uncover the glass globe, light the wick, and adjust the flame. Putting the globe back, I take a moment to admire the soft amber light it throws over the room.

The quiet light somehow reminds me of home. Suddenly I feel awful about what happened at dinner and I poke my head into the bedroom I'm sharing with Maddie. She lies on her bunk, snoring lightly as always, her social studies textbook open across her chest. I take my locket from my top drawer and gaze at the photos of my parents before clasping the chain around my neck. For a minute, I feel a little less alone.

Returning to the living room, I slide my English reading off the pile of my books on the table and open it to the assigned page. It's a novel from the 1800s by Charles Dickens called *A Tale of Two Cities*, set during the French Revolution. Most of the class hate it. They say it's too old-fashioned and hard to read. I find the writing style slow to wade through, too. But the book captured my interest from the very first line: "It was the best of times, it was the worst of times."

It was the best of times, it was the worst of times. I couldn't stop thinking about that. It seemed to fit my life so well. The world was in an awful state, and yet here I was, having the most exciting, most free, most interesting time ever.

I sit at the table and start to read by lamplight. I haven't gotten more than a page into it when I hear a key turn in the lock.

Everyone is here — so who could be coming in? I stand, alarmed, my open book still in my hand.

Rosie slips in the door and shuts it quietly.

"Rosie! You scared me!" I sigh as relief floods me. "I thought you were in your room. It's past curfew."

Rosie jumps at my voice and then slumps against the wall, putting her hands on her chest as though to quiet her pounding heart. "I know," she says with a breathless laugh. "I know. On my way back from the cafeteria I couldn't resist taking a walk in the woods. I just had to have some quiet alone time or I thought I'd go nuts."

"I know exactly how you feel," I agree. "It's hard always being with other people. That was starting to drive me nuts back in Chicago."

Rosie crosses to the couch and throws herself down onto it, one leg propped on the couch's arm, the other dragging onto the floor. "But then I was scared out of my mind trying to get back here without being seen. It was stupid. I'll never do something like that again." She propped herself on her elbow. "Hey, you got the lamp going. Cool."

There's an awkward pause as we both realize we never really talk, at least not outside of class.

"So, what do you think we'll be doing this weekend?" I ask, just to fill the empty space.

"Well, I don't know about the rest of you guys, but I thought I'd cruise the mall and take in a movie. Enjoy the air-conditioning," Rosie says, kicking off her sneakers.

This is totally *not* what I expected her to say! Imagine, Rosie Chavez making a joke!

"Maybe I'll come with you," I say, playing along. "I hear that a new fast-food place opened. You can get pizza, burgers, tacos, and ice cream all in one place."

"I wouldn't mind some of my mother's enchiladas suizas," Rosie says wistfully.

"That's a Mexican dish, isn't it?" I ask, recognizing the name from the local Mexican restaurant my parents, Maddie, and I used to like to go to.

"Yeah, it is."

"So you're Mexican?" I ask.

"My parents were born in Mexico. I was born in

Chicago. So that makes me American — as American as you."

"Yeah, of course," I say. "I was just curious. So . . . anyway . . . I know a good Mexican place we can go. How many enchiladas do you want to eat?"

"I don't know," Rosie says doubtfully. "I'd better not have too many. The other night I ate, like, an entire cow."

"Oh, me, too. I forgot," I say, keeping up the gag. "But after we eat, we can pop over to the health club for a game of tennis."

"Terrific idea," Rosie says loftily. "Let's just do that very thing."

We burst into laughter at the same moment. Even though it's not really funny, it's easier to joke about it.

Plus it feels really good to laugh.

"I see you're wearing your locket," Rosie observes. "Whose picture you got in there? A boyfriend?"

"No. My parents."

I expect her to make fun of me, but instead she asks to see the photos. Opening the locket, I show her.

"They look like they're nice," she says.

"The best," I reply.

"You're lucky," Rosie remarks.

There's a knock at the door — it's a Leaguer telling us to turn out the light and go to bed. "Sure thing," I say as I turn the dial to lower the wick into the oil, putting out the flame.

We're instantly plunged into near darkness. Only the strong moonlight that washes over everything allows us to find our way toward our rooms. "See ya tomorrow," I say softly to Rosie.

"Bright and early," she adds.

I tiptoe back into my and Maddie's room. Maddie is still asleep, which is fine with me. I'm not feeling so lonely anymore, and I don't want to get into a bunch of drama with her tonight. I don't want her to bring me down with all her negativity.

I've had a good day and a surprisingly nice night. But I'm exhausted and I just want to go to sleep.

Chapter 8

At breakfast next Saturday I stand by the buffet table wearing a stained white apron with straps that tie at my neck and a hem that falls past my knees. I'm about to scoop a large bowl of fruit salad into small white bowls when Mrs. Brewster stands at the front of the room and calls for silence. She has an important announcement.

"You girls will be spending this weekend in very special classes," Mrs. Brewster says.

A low murmur of disappointed grumbling travels across the cafeteria. We've been so busy this week that everyone is exhausted and looking forward to some time off.

I have mixed feelings, though. I'm tired, too, and wouldn't mind some time to just chill. Yet I lean forward, interested to hear what Mrs. Brewster will say next. Country Manor is so full of wonderful surprises.

"These special classes all involve outdoor survival skills. Your class assignments are listed on the bulletin board there by the door," Mrs. Brewster tells us. "Check for your classes after you finish eating your breakfast."

There's no way I can wait until I eat before checking my class assignment. I'm way too excited. Going directly to the board, I give a little fist pump of excitement when I see that I'm to report to the pool.

Yes! I'm finally going to see the famous CMS Olympic-sized pool.

I rush through my kitchen chores and then hurry to the suite to grab my purple tank suit and put it on under shorts and a T-shirt. I meet Maddie in the bathroom when I go for a towel. "I'm going to the pool," I say excitedly. "What class do you have?"

"Tent raising or some stupid thing like that," Maddie answers sourly. "It's in the forest."

"Are you okay?" I ask.

"Fine," Maddie mumbles.

"Are you sure?" I press.

"Yeah, yeah. Whatever." Maddie waves me away. "Go. You don't want to be late."

"You're right," I agree, already moving out of the bathroom with one of our plain white towels in my hand. "Have fun at your class."

"I'm sure it will be a blast," she grumbles.

As I hurry out of the dorms and toward the pool, I wonder why Maddie can't just get into the spirit of things. What's got her so bugged?

The first floor of the pool building is a changing area, an expansive room lined with lockers. I notice that no one has put a lock on any of the lockers and, at first, I hesitate. What if someone takes my stuff? Back in my old school, theft was a big problem.

But then I rethink it.

What do I have left that anyone would want to steal? And even if they did steal my sneakers or something, I'd spot them eventually.

So I quickly undress down to my bathing suit, step into my flip-flops, and throw my towel around my neck.

I see a sign with an arrow and the word POOL. I follow it down some dark, dungeon-like steps.

The sounds of girls' voices vibrating with that particular pool echo effect tells me I'm getting close. When I pass through the entrance at the bottom of the steps I feel a rush of excitement. There it is — aqua and shimmering. No lap ropes disturb the serenely sparkling field of blue.

It's completely as I'd pictured it.

But a second glance reveals something totally unexpected.

Canoes! Four of them are lined up at the three-foot end. Two girls are seated in each canoe. Several more girls sit on the edge, their legs in the water.

Devi is in a blue tank suit. Emmanuelle is there, too, also in a bathing suit, assisting her. Emmanuelle smiles at me when I enter.

Devi stands at the pool's edge. She wears water shoes and has a whistle around her neck and a clipboard in her hand. "You're late," she states evenly when I approach.

"I apologize to you and the class," I say. "It won't happen again." In the last week I've learned that this is the expected response to the charge of lateness. That morning I was delayed because, after breakfast, the girl I was working with in the kitchen, Anne Abadi, had cramps and had to sit down. That left me to finish both of our work. There was no use in saying this to Devi. No excuses, no matter how valid, are acceptable.

And, the fact is, I am not actually late at all. I am exactly on time. But at CMS, on time is late. We are expected to be at every class and event five minutes — ten minutes is even better — early. This rule makes Maddie nuts. "You're either on time or you're not," she insists. I see the point, though. When the class or whatever starts, we're already focused and ready to go.

I join the girls at the end of the pool and listen as Devi picks up an oar. "If you are seated in the back of the canoe, you are in the stern. That makes you the helmswoman, which means you are in charge of steering. The person at the front, called the bow, is simply providing power forward. The first thing the helmswoman

96

must know about steering the boat is how to do a J-stroke."

Devi demonstrates how to do it. Then the crew in the four canoes goes out into the pool to try it. There is a lot of laughter as the girls collide with one another; it's clear that keeping a canoe on course is not as simple as it looks. After those girls practice, another group takes its turn.

Finally, it's my turn to get into a canoe. Getting into the tippy boat is not easy. I have to keep my weight low, and even then the canoe rocks from side to side.

I'm assigned to sit in the back to steer. While Teresa Balmer gets into the bow, I can't resist dangling my arms into the cool water. It's so refreshing I can almost cry with delight. This pool water brings back so many good memories — happy days spent swimming with my family, the thrill of competing when I was on the team.

At the end of four hours, we've learned to steer, turn, back up, hold the canoe in a stationary position, and bring a canoe into a narrow docking space.

The last lesson is the most fun. We take the canoes into the middle of the pool, with three girls in the boats this time, and the middle girl stands up. She bounces until the canoe is rocking so violently that it tips and we are all thrown into the water. This, we are told, is called capsizing. We are then taught how to right the boat once more by very quickly swimming back to it before it takes on too much water and sinks. We station ourselves on one side and, all at once, press our weight down until the opposite side rises.

It's sort of thrilling when the opposite end starts to come up, dumping a torrent of water on all of us. Then it plops over with a tremendous splat, spraying us even more. Of course, the trick then becomes to make sure the canoe doesn't float away on its own before we can climb back in.

I'm smiling from ear to ear as I hurry back to my room to change for lunch. Even though I didn't get to swim, learning to canoe is the most fun I've had in . . . maybe ever. No kidding! To be out here where the air is clean — at least much cleaner than in Chicago — and schoolwork is combined with outdoor skills is like a dream to me. It's as if CMS was designed just for me.

• • • •

On Saturday night I put down my book to answer a brisk knock at our door.

"Lights out, girls!" Evelyn cries, smiling in her new League gear — night-vision goggles in her bag, Student League pin on her collar.

I excitedly drag her inside. "Let's see them!" I cry.

"No. It's against regulations," Evelyn says, trying to be serious and official.

Rosie looks up from *A Tale of Two Cities*, which she is desperately trying to finish before all the classes have a test on Monday. I can't believe they're expecting us to finish the whole book in a week. "Oh, come on!" Rosie pleads. "Let's see them."

"Please," I beg. "You said you would."

"No, she didn't," says Maddie from her spot on the couch where she's reading her social studies text.

"See?" Evelyn insists. "I didn't."

"Please," I repeat.

Evelyn shifts from foot to foot indecisively.

"Pretty please," I whine.

"Oh, all right," Evelyn gives in with a big smile. She reaches into the canvas bag she carries over her shoulder and pulls them out.

"Turn out the lamp!" I cry as I stretch the rubber strap over my head and adjust the goggles over my eyes.

"I'm trying to read here," Maddie complains to Rosie, who plunges us into darkness when she douses the lamp's wick into the oil.

I can see everything! It's all gray, of course, with patches of red here and splotches of green there. Just the same, I can see them all fine. "This is amazing," I say. "I feel like a soldier or something."

"Let me try," Rosie requests. She's trying to be cool, I can tell. But she's excited.

"Come get them," I say, knowing full well she can't see me.

"Very funny," she replies. "Bring them to me. You're the one who can see."

Moving as silently as I can, I sneak over to where Maddie is on the couch and poke her in the arm.

Maddie shrieks.

"Quiet!" Evelyn says in a hushed, worried voice. "You'll get me into trouble."

"Sorry," Maddie apologizes peevishly. "Some idiot nearly scared me to death by poking me in the dark. And I'm pretty sure I know who it was."

"Can't you take a joke?" I ask, annoyed. Can't she have fun for two minutes?

"Give me the goggles," Rosie prods.

"Yeah, give them to her," Evelyn says. "I have to get going."

I find Rosie and take hold of her arm. "Here," I say, handing her the goggles.

"Whoa," Rosie says once she has them on. "I *need* a pair of these. Totally must have them."

After a few minutes she offers them to Maddie. "Want to try?"

"Nah, it's okay," Maddie declines halfheartedly. "I don't want Evelyn to get into trouble."

Rosie lights the oil lamp again and takes off the goggles. "Thanks, Evelyn," she says, handing them back.

"Okay, guys, gotta go," Evelyn says as she returns the goggles to her bag. "That lamp has to be turned off in five minutes," she adds.

"Yes, ma'am," I say with a little salute.

"Rule number twenty-eight of the League code: no special favors for friends or family," Evelyn says lightly as she crosses to Maddie. With a smile, she delivers a comforting pat on Maddie's back.

Maddie returns Evelyn's smile with a look of genuine affection. This surprises me. I hadn't realized the two of them had grown so close. I suppose I shouldn't be surprised, though. I haven't been paying much attention to Maddie since the evening she walked out of the cafeteria.

Has Maddie been confiding in Evelyn?

Actually, it makes sense. Maddie hates CMS and Evelyn thinks it's all some evil conspiracy. Naturally they'd have a lot to talk about.

A jolt of jealousy hits me but it quickly passes.

Fine, I think, *it's about time she makes some other friends and doesn't rely on me for everything.*

• • •

Sunday is a half day of classes, morning only, but I have to be up by four thirty for my second week of kitchen staff. I hope the next time I pull this assignment, they'll give me lunch or dinner duty. Getting up every morning before dawn is a killer.

"Why are you up?" Maddie mumbles, rolling over in her top bunk. "It's Sunday."

"You still have to eat breakfast on Sunday," I remind her.

"At five thirty in the morning?" Maddie grumbles. "Why can't they give us a break? Haven't they ever heard of the *weekend* in this hellhole? I'm skipping breakfast. I need to sleep."

"You're not allowed to skip any meals," I remind her.

Pulling the pillow over her head, she makes a sound that is halfway between a scream and a grunt. Kind of a roar of deep displeasure, I suppose. "This place is the pits," she declares before rolling over to face the wall.

"Sorry you think so," I mutter as I leave the room, and

hurry down the stairs to begin my trek through the early-morning fog.

Today Anne Abadi is feeling much better, so we have a full crew and we get out on time. I arrive at the pool a full ten minutes early, as expected. In the water, four canoes once again float together side by side. I wonder what more there is to learn about canoeing. Almost as though she's read my mind, Devi says, "Now that you know the basics, the most important thing is for you all to practice. And that's what we'll be doing today."

We're split into three-girl teams and given a series of challenges. The team that rows to the opposite end of the pool, switches positions without capsizing, turns, rows to the center, then stands up to tip the canoe, rights it again, and rows back in the best time, wins. Devi and Emmanuelle hold up their stopwatches to indicate they will be timing the event.

My team can't stop giggling during the capsizing part, but everyone is shouting and laughing on all the teams, and we come in second. I have even more fun than I did on Saturday.

And actually being in the water is so amazing! To be surrounded by the flowing coolness — to float, weightless! It's something I worried I would never experience again, but here I am.

During the capsize part, I take a minute to duck below the surface. A world of water — clean, beautiful water. The lost world of water! It isn't a dream; it's Country Manor.

Heading back to lunch with Sara, one of the girls from my canoe, I meet Rosie, her tall tennis friend, and the gymnast with the long black ponytail. I don't know what to expect. Will Rosie snub me now that she's with her sporty friends?

"Hey." Rosie greets me with a smile. "Look what we did all morning." She and her two friends each hold up a jumble of rope tied in a bunch of different ways.

I think they must have been in some arts-and-crafts macramé class. "Nice," I say uneasily. "What are they?"

The three of them laugh at my confusion, but not in a mean way. "They're knots," Rosie explains.

"Every kind of knot known to humankind," adds the tall girl.

Rosie introduces me. The tennis girl is Mary Jensen and the ponytailed girl is Chui-lian Lee. "You can call me Chewy," she says. "Everyone does."

"This is Louisa, my one cool roommate I was telling you about," Rosie adds.

I introduce them to Sara, feeling flattered and happy at Rosie's description of me. But I also feel like I should stick up for Evelyn and Maddie. When the other girls head back to their rooms and it's just me and Rosie, I tell her, "Evelyn and Maddie are great. You just have to get to know them."

"You know, for twins, you and Maddie aren't that much alike. But she must be okay, I guess," Rosie allows. "Still, you have to admit that Evelyn is a kook."

"She let you wear her night-vision goggles," I remind her.

"True. She means well, I guess. But she's still living on a totally different planet."

Chapter 9

I walk to lunch with Rosie, and we meet Mary and Chewy on the way. Their stories about knot-tying class are hilarious. I can't stop laughing when Chewy tells how she tied her fingers up while trying to lash two branches together.

When we walk into the cafeteria, I realize I have a problem. "Come on over and sit with us," Mary invites me. But Evelyn and Maddie are already sitting together. Evelyn sees me and waves.

"I should really sit with Evelyn and Maddie," I say.

"Why?" Rosie asks. "You don't have to."

"Can we invite them to join us?" I ask.

Rosie, Chewy, and Mary look at one another, their expressions reluctant.

"They're really nice," I press.

"Okay. Ask them," Rosie relents.

I hurry to where Evelyn and Maddie are sitting. They have their heads together. When I get closer, I realize they have a map unfolded on their laps between them. "Hey, guys," I greet them. "Want to sit with Rosie and two of her friends?"

They look up from the map and stare at me as if I'd just spoken to them in another language.

"They want *us* to sit with *them*?" Maddie asks. Her baffled tone implies that this makes absolutely no sense. And I can kind of see her point.

"Yeah. Come on," I say. "It will do good things for our . . . you know . . . our status. They're cool."

"We're cool," Evelyn counters.

Not really, I think. But I don't say it, of course. "But you'll like them. You'll see," I say.

"I don't think so," Maddie insists. "I don't know how you got them to invite us, but I'm fine right here, thanks."

My temper is rising. She can be so stubborn!

"Thanks, but we're okay," Evelyn agrees in a nicer tone. "We're kind of into this map thing."

"What are you doing?" I ask.

Evelyn lowers her voice. "Our cover story is that we're preparing for the geography part of a social studies test, but we're really trying to figure out where the heck we are." She opens her closed palm to reveal her compass. "We're trying to work it out using this."

That sounds pretty impossible to me. And so not worth the effort, either.

"You go, though," Evelyn says. "I don't think this is your kind of thing. No offense."

"I'm not offended. You're right; I'm not that into it," I agree. "See you guys later."

My emotions are mixed as I head for the table where Rosie, Chewy, and Mary are sitting with a few other members of their athletic crowd. Even though it wasn't a big scene, I feel like what just happened was a big deal. It was a rift between Maddie and me, and it feels kind of permanent. All at the same time, I'm super-relieved that they didn't want to join us, and yet I am already lonely for Maddie and even Evelyn, too. It's as if I've moved into some kind of future from which there's no going back.

It's just lunch! I scold myself. *Don't make so much out of it.* With that thought, I push Maddie and Evelyn out of my head and sit down with my new friends. "They say thanks, but they were in the middle of studying for some test."

Rosie, Mary, and Chewy all brighten. "Oh. Okay, good," Rosie says. Then she goes on to introduce me to the rest of her friends.

We're all free for the rest of the afternoon, so I spend it with Rosie and her crowd. We hang out by the lake and talk about CMS. These girls feel like I do — they love it here. It's everything they could have hoped for. "I'm getting so strong," Rosie says, flexing her right biceps.

Mary punches the hard calf muscle of her leg. "Look at this," she says. "I can't wait to play tennis again. I bet my game will be stronger than ever."

I realize that I've also become more toned than I've ever been. It feels good to be strong and to be learning so many new things. A new confidence is growing inside me.

Across the lake, a group of boys heads out of the forest and into their main building. Seized by a sudden boldness, I stand and wave with a broad, sweeping gesture. They're pretty far away, but several heads turn in my direction. One boy returns my wave.

The other girls start giggling and waving, too.

Several more boys wave back.

Their teacher notices and reprimands them, hurrying them along into the building. We all dissolve into fits of laughter. "I can't believe you did that!" Chewy says.

"I was only being friendly," I reply.

Around six thirty, Rosie and I head back to our dorm together. "What was it like to be in a coma?" I ask Rosie.

"What do you mean?"

"I heard you on the bus that first day," I tell her.

"Oh, that," she says. She smiles softly to herself. "I was never in a coma," Rosie whispers. "I just said that to get their attention. They all thought they were so cool with their big sports injuries. Don't tell anyone."

"I won't," I agree. "You're too much. You became their leader as soon as you said that. You know that, right?"

Rosie nods, pleased by my words. "Do you think so?"

"Yeah, definitely," I affirm.

"You have to know how to manage people," Rosie says. "That's a survival skill, too. It's probably the most important one of all. If you don't get to the inside of a group right away, you could find yourself on the outside, like . . ." Her voice trails off.

"Like who?" I press. The moment I speak I know the answer. She was about to say, *like Evelyn and Maddie.*

"Like nobody," Rosie covers quickly. "I was just saying . . . it could happen to a person."

When we get to the suite, both Maddie and Evelyn are in their separate rooms reading. Rosie and I chat a little more in the main room and then go to our rooms at about seven forty-five.

Maddie puts her book down when I enter. "What did you do today?" she asks.

"Nothing, just hung with Rosie and her friends," I answer as I take my nightshirt from the drawer. I am about to tell her about what happened with the boys across the lake, but think better of it. I don't want her to make some sour comment that will ruin it for me. "What did you do?" I ask instead.

"Not much. I think we figured out where we are, though — right smack on the Canadian border in Minnesota," she says.

"That means that winters here are going to be hard," I note.

"Not only that," Maddie says, getting up onto her elbow. "Evelyn says that the Alliance is very strong in Canada. Alliance groups have gotten into every sector of the Canadian government."

"That's Canada's problem," I say, slipping the night-shirt over my head. I'll take a shower in the morning, I decide. I'm just suddenly exhausted. Early kitchen duty is really tiring me out.

"Yeah, but we're right on the *border*," Maddie says again.

"Don't let Evelyn get to you," I say, enjoying the soft comfort of my bunk.

"Doesn't that concern you even a little?" Maddie asks. Judging from her agitated tone, I can tell it obviously concerns *her*.

"No, not at all," I state, yawning. "Sorry; I have to sleep. I can't talk about this for another minute. Good night."

I don't know if Maddie answers me or not because my eyes slide shut and I'm instantly asleep, already dreaming of Monday, eager for the new day to begin.

Monday after breakfast Mrs. Brewster tells all of us to stay for her big announcement: our first overnight trip will be this upcoming weekend!

Rosie and I squeal with excitement, hugging each other. "Do you feel ready for this?" I ask.

"I do. I think so. Yes," Rosie replies.

"Me, too," I say, though I'm not really so sure. We've been training for this all week. And it's not like I have to know all the outdoor things. We all have our areas of

114

skill and we'll have to work together as a team, I imagine.

I run into Evelyn and Maddie on my way to English class. "So? Are you guys psyched for the overnight?" I ask eagerly.

"Oh, yeah, way psyched," Maddie replies in a sarcastically dull monotone.

I sigh, but otherwise I ignore her remark.

"It could be interesting," Evelyn allows. "But get this, when I was on rounds last night I heard some of the teachers talking. This trip is happening earlier than was originally planned. The staff moved it forward because they're worried about bad weather sooner than expected."

"Okay. So?" I say. "I don't see the big deal."

"Think!" Evelyn scolds. "They *know the weather.*"

"Which means what?" I ask.

"Which means they obviously have a radio or TV or something, somewhere in this place," Evelyn says knowingly.

"Unless they have a psychic on staff," Maddie jokes. "A Canadian weather psychic."

Evelyn laughs. "Oh, that's funny! The Alliance ESP Division!"

Suddenly I remember about the Canadian food. "I've been meaning to mention something to you, Evelyn," I begin. "You asked me to keep my eyes open in the kitchen, remember?"

"Uh-huh," Evelyn agrees, still laughing.

"Well, the only thing I noticed is that all our food comes from a Canadian company."

Evelyn stops laughing. "Are you kidding?"

"No. Really."

Evelyn takes out a little notepad — a paper one — that she has in her pocket. She flips it open and then takes out her pen.

"A lot of different Canadian companies, or just one?" Evelyn asks.

"It's all from the same place," I tell her. "Some place called NutriCorp. It uses a big Canadian maple leaf on its logo."

Evelyn writes this down in her notebook.

"Do you think that's important?" I ask.

"Who knows? It might be," Evelyn answers. "It shows a connection between CMS and someone in Canada."

"Couldn't it just be the closest place for CMS to have food delivered from?" I challenge.

Sasha, our English teacher, comes by. "Get to class, girls," she says briskly.

We take the test on *A Tale of Two Cities* that morning. We're asked to compare the time of the French Revolution to our times. I smile when I see the question because I've already given this some thought.

Once we've handed in our papers, Sasha collects our Dickens novels. "Evelyn and Louisa, please take out the novels you'll find in the back of the cabinet by the door. Pass them out among the class."

In the cabinet, Evelyn and I find a stack of paperback books, all the same. *Julie of the Wolves* by Jean Craighead George. The books themselves are yellowed and frayed. And I know it was written a while back.

As soon as I hand Maddie her copy, she raises her hand. "Sasha," she says when she's acknowledged, "isn't

117

this book kind of young for us? I read it in the sixth grade."

"If you read it that long ago, then you'll most likely need to refresh your memory and reread it," Sasha says.

"But why are we reading such a young book?" Maddie presses.

"The theme of surviving by living in accord with the natural world is very relevant to your work here at Country Manor School," Sasha explains.

Maddie and Evelyn exchange darting glances of concern. And even I — excited as I am about the overnight — worry that we might be expected to befriend wolves over the weekend. At CMS, anything is possible.

Chapter 10

Devi holds up a cluster of small purple berries. "If you found these in the woods, would you eat them?" she asks the eight of us sitting on the ground at her feet. We're just outside the forest surrounding the school.

Alice Abbott raises her hand and speaks when Devi nods to her. "I would. They look to me like small grapes, or maybe blueberries."

"You're right and you're wrong," Devi says. "They're elderberries. Are they edible?"

My arm shoots up. "Yes," I answer, eager to show I've been studying.

"The whole plant?" Devi questions me.

"Yes," I reply.

"Wrong," Devi says. "The berries are good to eat. The roots are poisonous."

There is so much to know and I've been working so hard. But what we need to learn seems endless. I don't know how I'll ever master this information, but I want to know it all.

The more academic morning teachers don't seem to mind that we're half-asleep because the afternoon teachers are working us so hard. I'm up until lights-out every night as I pore over the manual on laying a trail someone else can follow (by putting down different types of markers, including making a gash in a tree called an ax blaze and building rock formations called cairns).

And this is the week I discover that I have really good aim.

At the rifle range, I hit the target every time. No more wild shots that go off into the woods. I've gotten used to aiming low, to compensate for the kickback on the rifle.

Rosie is still the star of the range. But when I hit my first bull's-eye cluster with one bullet dead center,

I'm most proud when she gives me a thumbs-up. "You'll be giving me some real competition soon," she remarks.

"Count on it," I reply with a smile, meaning it. My goal is to someday be as good a shot as she is. Maybe even better.

Archery lessons are a little more challenging — just getting the bow and arrow into position without it all tumbling to the ground takes several tries. And my first shots are crazy. One goes straight up and makes everyone duck for cover when it lands. The next couple fly off into the forest somewhere (probably scaring a few squirrels half to death).

By the end of the first day, I have bruises from where the string of the bow hits on the inside of my left arm when I release it incorrectly. Devi, who is teaching the class, gets me a leather armguard, which helps.

My fingers take a beating, too. When the arrow isn't placed quite right, its guide feathers, at the bottom of the arrow — which only look like feathers but are actually a kind of stiff nylon — slice my fingers. It really hurts.

Like a paper cut, which I've also been getting a lot of lately, only worse.

By the end of Thursday, though, I'm hitting the target regularly. I feel satisfied every time I hear that *whap–thunk* sound of my arrow being released and hitting the mark. At the very end of class, I hit my first bull's-eye.

"Congratulations," Devi says to me as she pulls my arrow out of the target. "A bull's-eye after only four days of shooting is pretty impressive."

I can't stop smiling. I'm so proud of myself. It's a great feeling.

Thursday night I tack my paper archery target up on our bedroom door. Maddie comes by and studies it, and then turns to me. "Wow," she says. "That's amazing."

I'm in my lower bunk, looking at the pictures of Mom and Dad in my locket. "Thanks," I say. "Who knew how much I'd love shooting at things?"

"I can see why. You're good at it," Maddie says.

It surprises me that she didn't make some critical remark about archery being stupid or useless. "How are you doing in your classes?" I ask, a touch of caution in my voice. I miss talking to her, but it's hard not to set off her negativity these days.

"Okay, I guess," Maddie says. "I can finally pitch a tent that doesn't fall down around my head. And my campfires don't fizzle out after five minutes anymore."

I laugh lightly. "Well, that's good."

"Yeah, I guess," Maddie says. "I still can't hit a target for anything, though."

"Maybe I could help you sometime. Rosie is really good at shooting. We could ask her if she'd —"

"No, thanks," Maddie says quickly, and I can't help but brace myself for some sour comment. "But I'd like it if you'd help me."

Phew. Maybe this is a good time to get through to her, finally. Putting my locket back under my shirt, I sit up. "Listen, Maddie," I begin. "I'm sorry we haven't been spending so much time together. It's just that I really love it here, and you . . . don't."

"I know. This whole *elite leaders of tomorrow* thing, it weirds me out," Maddie says.

"Don't take it so seriously," I advise her. "It's just

something they say to make us feel important. Just think of all the cool stuff we get to do that we'd never — *ever* — have the chance to do if we were at home. Where else would we learn all this? Nowhere!"

"But that's just it — why do they have us out here in the middle of *nowhere*?" Maddie asks.

"You're starting to sound like Evelyn," I point out.

"Really, though. Why are we so far away from everything? We can't even get any mail!"

"Because this is one of the only places in the country where nature hasn't been totally wrecked by pollution and the War," I say.

"Why is it so secretive?" Maddie pushes.

"For our safety!"

Maddie shakes her head sadly. "I don't believe that."

"Why not?"

"I can't explain it. I just don't." Maddie sighs.

"Could it be, really, that you're just homesick . . . for your own mom and dad?" I ask gently.

Tears well in Maddie's eyes as she nods. "I miss them an awful lot."

"I miss my parents, too," I admit. "But they're fine, and your parents are fine. And right now we have such a cool life here, Maddie. Why can't we just enjoy it for what it is?"

Maddie sits on the edge of my bed. "What is it, though? It confuses me."

"I just told you! It's a great chance to learn some cool stuff, get a good education, have fun, and make some awesome new friends."

"I don't want awesome new friends," Maddie insists, wiping the wetness from her eyes.

"You've met Evelyn," I remind her.

"Yeah, Evelyn is great," Maddie admits. "But I don't like that you've made great new friends. At least, you think they're great."

I know she's talking about Rosie and her crowd. "They like CMS, too, like I do," I explain.

Maddie nods, and then sniffs. "I know."

A rush of guilt suddenly hits me like a bomb. Maddie's been homesick, lonely, and confused. And what did I do? I got mad at her. I deserted her.

"I'm sorry, Maddie," I say sincerely. "I've been kind of a jerk."

Without looking at me, Maddie shakes her head. "It's okay. I've been a pain."

"What a pair of twins we make," I say with a sad laugh, "a jerk and a pain."

Maddie lifts her head and laughs, despite her blood-shot eyes. "Yeah, some pair."

Putting my arm around her shoulders, I squeeze tight. "Want to be friends again?"

"I would like that," Maddie agrees.

Taking my arm from her shoulder, I hold out my hand. "Friends?" I ask.

Maddie shakes my hand. "Friends," she confirms with a smile.

Reaching around, I hug her tight. Maddie and I are friends again and I am so happy. I've missed her.

On Friday our morning academic classes are called off so we can prepare for our overnight. "You girls will be divided into teams according to suite," Mrs. Brewster announces that morning after breakfast.

That's fine with me. Now that Maddie and I are friends again, I realize I really like my suite. I think we make a good group.

After Mrs. Brewster dismisses us, I have to finish my kitchen staff duties. It's my last week! No more four thirty for me! It's now going to feel luxurious to sleep until five fifteen!

Everyone has left the cafeteria by the time I finish. Just before I go, I tear the maple-leaf NutriCorp logo off a can of whole tomatoes and stick it into my jeans pocket for Evelyn.

"Here," I say as I walk into our dorm room and hand the label to Evelyn, "some hard evidence for you."

Maddie, Evelyn, and Rosie are all in the main living room with their clothes spread all over, along with ground covers, sleeping bags, mess kits, and other camping gear that's been distributed to each student.

Rosie shoots me a dark look of disapproval, but I ignore her.

Evelyn takes the scrap of label from me and gapes at it as though I've just handed her a diamond necklace. "This is great," she says, awestruck. "Thanks!"

"No big deal," I say.

"What are you actually going to do with that?" Rosie asks Evelyn. "I mean, *really*?"

"I'm not sure yet," Evelyn replies defensively. "It's real evidence, like Louisa says."

"I was kind of kidding," I tell her.

"Just the same, it *is* evidence," Evelyn insists.

Rosie rolls her dark eyes and sighs. "Whatever you say." She doesn't even try to hide the fact that she thinks Evelyn is completely out of her mind.

"I better start packing," I say, partly to change the subject. "I see you guys are way ahead of me." I head into my bedroom and find my backpack in the closet. "I don't know how all this stuff is going to fit in this thing," I call back over my shoulder.

"It isn't easy," Maddie replies.

"You can do it," Rosie says. "I'm already done."

On Saturday I awaken before dawn to the sounds of my dorm mates stumbling around in the dark — this early we can only light one candle per room, and it isn't enough light by a long shot. I hear Evelyn shout as she stubs her toe on the corner of her bunk.

Her cry somehow brings me fully awake. "I have to get to the kitchen!" I shout, throwing off my covers. "I've overslept!" I only have fifteen minutes to get there.

Grabbing my backpack, I hurry ahead to the cafeteria and discover a pleasant surprise. "The teachers are helping the kitchen staff prepare breakfast today," Devi tells me. "We need to hurry things along this morning."

Breakfast is granola, milk, and fruit. For the first time ever, Rosie sits with Evelyn, Maddie, and me. Now that our dorm is a team, I guess she feels that her loyalty lies with us. I appreciate that. Rosie is a team player, for sure. If we have any chance of doing well at all, it will be because Rosie is with us. To be honest, I know I'll be her second in command, a co-captain.

"Each team will receive a topographical map, a compass, and a destination to reach by lunchtime," Mrs. Brewster tells us while we eat. "At that destination you will receive instructions. You'll have thirty-six hours before you have to return with a certain leaf, water, and dirt samples," she continues. "An automatic A will be given to anyone who hunts and kills an animal bigger than a squirrel."

"What?" I whisper in disbelief. "Kill?" I really hope I've misunderstood something here. "I refuse to kill an animal. I won't," I say to no one in particular.

Mrs. Brewster shoots a disapproving, warning glance in my direction. I shut up.

Then she goes on, assigning locations for each group to meet before hiking out into the forest behind the school. We're going to hike ten miles in before setting up our campsite. For the first time, my excitement is giving way to nervousness.

"Was she serious about us killing animals?" I ask as soon as Mrs. Brewster dismisses us.

Rosie answers me in an annoyed tone. "What did you think we were learning sharpshooting for?"

"Not for that," Maddie insists. "Killing animals is gross."

"Do you like to eat, Maddie?" Rosie replies.

Evelyn covers her face with her hands. "I can't deal with this," she mumbles.

"Come on, you guys," Rosie says sternly. "We have to do whatever they ask us to do. You can't wimp out."

I can tell that Rosie is rising to take charge of our group, just as I expected. I feel obliged to back her up. "We'll do whatever it takes, Rosie. You don't have to worry about us." I turn to Evelyn and Maddie. "Right?"

"Yeah," Evelyn mumbles.

"Sure," Maddie murmurs.

I understand how they feel. But I'm working hard to disguise my worries.

Rosie heads to the table where the maps and compasses are laid out, and picks out one of each for our group. When she returns, she also has a nylon bag that holds the camp lunches — the only food the staff have prepared for us. We don our backpacks and then head for our assigned meeting place at the edge of the forest.

I'm surprised to see that there are two other suite sets of girls waiting there, as well.

"We're a team of twelve. That's what Devi told us," says Anne Abadi, who has her dark hair in two braids and a red bandanna covering her head. She reports this to Rosie, as though she recognizes Rosie as the leader without being told.

Rosie makes a quick study of the group. From the seriousness in her darting eyes, I can tell she's assessing them, sizing them up, thinking about what she knows about each one and making an educated guess about their strengths and weaknesses. Finally, she nods to herself before clapping her hands sharply. "Okay, let's get going," she says briskly. "We have to make camp at a spot called Eagles Aerie."

I'm surprised when Rosie hands our group's compass to Evelyn.

"I know you're good with a compass," she says to her. "I'll read the map and you point us in the right direction."

If anyone from the other groups minds the way Rosie is giving orders, they clearly don't want to say so out loud.

Rosie unfolds the map and looks it over for a moment. "Start us off in a northwesterly direction," she tells Evelyn.

Peering down at the compass, Evelyn turns in a slow circle before pointing into the forest. "That way," she says.

"Cool. Head out," Rosie commands.

Everyone happily falls in line — except Maddie. I hurry to her side. "Come on. You can't hang behind like this. You have to keep up."

"I don't like this," Maddie frets.

"Why not?"

"For one thing, I don't feel like taking orders from Ms. Bossy Chavez all weekend."

The others are getting farther and farther away from us. I take hold of Maddie's elbow. "We have to catch up," I say.

"Oh, all right," Maddie reluctantly agrees. Running at a jog, we catch up with the back of the line.

"Quit poking along back there," Rosie orders from the front. "Keep up."

Maddie tips her head toward me and speaks softly. "Why do you like her, Louisa?"

Slowing down, I create a little space between us and the next-nearest person in the line so we won't be overheard. "You should get to know Rosie better," I suggest. "I didn't like her at first, either. She's better one-on-one than she is in a group."

"If you say so," Maddie allows, but I know she doesn't believe me.

Chapter 11

As we head deeper and deeper into the forest, it becomes increasingly difficult to navigate through the thick pines. The trees grow more closely together and the trail we're on becomes overgrown with bushes and thorny brambles. The overhead thickness of the pines doesn't allow in much sunlight and the forest quickly seems shadowy, even though I know it can't even be noon yet.

"Break!" Rosie calls when we near a narrow, quickly flowing creek.

"Can we drink from the creek?" asks a girl named Carole Osterly, who I know is from Anne Abadi's suite.

"Better not," Rosie says. "If that lake is really polluted, then the streams feeding it might also be bad."

"That lake isn't polluted and neither is this stream," Evelyn objects. "Look how clear it is, and it's running fast."

Her furrowed brow shows that Rosie doesn't appreciate being challenged. "Suit yourself. But I don't want to know about it when you're sick tonight. Don't even wake me up. My advice is to sip from your water bottles if you're thirsty."

No one drinks from the creek.

About an hour later, Maddie and three other girls sit on some boulders we're passing to rest.

"No sitting!" Rosie barks at them. "Don't you remember anything from outdoor skills class? Your muscles will cramp and it will be harder to continue. If you have to rest, lean against a tree. It will cool you down and keep your muscles stretched."

Rolling her eyes, Maddie rises and puts her back against the wide trunk of a pine. "Great, now my shirt is full of pine sap," she complains.

I also lean against a tree and, actually, I don't mind it. I'm enjoying the moss that cushions my shoulder and cheek as I lean into the trunk of a towering pine. It's cooling and soft.

Rosie moves into an area of dappled sunlight that's found its way through the canopy of pine needles above. She uses that light to study her map. "We need to go due west now," Rosie tells Evelyn. "By the way, nice job navigating so far."

"Thanks," Evelyn says, and she begins another slow turn, her focus on the needle of the compass in her hand.

I catch Maddie's eyes and nod significantly, as if to say, *See, Rosie can be nice.*

Maddie shrugs and I read her skeptical expression. *So she was a little nice; so what?*

We walk through the forest again for what feels like a very long time. Without even being able to see the sun, it's hard to tell exactly how long.

At a certain point, our path becomes so steep that it's hard for us to breathe. Everyone, even Rosie, is panting hard when we ascend to a rocky break in the forest. "We're above the tree line," Rosie announces.

The shadowy gloom gives way to bright sunshine and a crystal-blue sky as we scramble over rocks, leaving the pines behind. The sun is directly overhead in the sky by the time Evelyn says, "Eagles Aerie should be right up there."

Squinting against the bright light, I see a flat, rocky, open space. It seems to be the very top of a mountain.

That final ascent to Eagles Aerie is brutally steep, with small stones that slide out from under our sneakers as we make our way to the summit. I slip once and skin my knee on a rock. Despite my aching muscles, I start to feel excited — we're so close now! And yet so far away from anything else. I've never seen this much wilderness in my life, and now I'm completely surrounded by it, with only myself and the other girls to rely on.

It's exhilarating.

Rosie reaches the top first and begins searching around for something. "Help me find the instructions Mrs. Brewster said would be here," she tells us.

We begin turning over rocks and looking around the

base of boulders. I check the roots of one of the scrubby, wind-stripped trees that grow all around.

"Here it is!" Carole cries. She digs into a pile of stones and produces a small red notebook.

Evelyn watches over Carole's shoulder as she opens the book. Evelyn's lips press together in distress and she gazes up at the rest of us unhappily. "It's just an empty notebook," she announces, confused.

Rosie takes the book from Carole and fans through the pages. Then she closes it and opens it again, this time to the first page. "'Each team member must sign in. Then seek further instructions,'" she reads. Rosie looks up at us with a worried expression. "Did anyone bring a pen?"

Each girl looks to the one nearest her with questioning eyes. "I did," Evelyn says with a note of reluctance as she takes a pen from the pocket of her shorts. I'm sure her little notebook is in her shorts pocket, too. Evelyn would never go on a trip like this without being able to take notes. She probably didn't want everyone to know this, though.

Taking the pen from Evelyn, Rosie offers it to the others. "Everyone sign in or you won't get credit for reaching the top," she says. "While you're waiting to sign, look around for anything with instructions written on it."

"Can we eat lunch up here?" asks a girl with short hair named Erica Felstein. "They packed food for us, didn't they?"

Rosie opens the nylon bag she's been carrying. Taking out what looks like a butter sandwich, she digs deeper. She takes out a large metal canteen and twelve paper cups. "That's it," she reports unhappily.

"Are you joking?" Anne Abadi cries.

Rosie shakes her head and empties out the bag on a flat rock. "Twelve butter sandwiches and a canteen of water."

"After all this hiking and climbing they give us bread and water!?" Maddie shouts indignantly. "I don't believe this place. It's inhuman!"

But it's better than nothing. Still standing, we devour our thin sandwiches and drink the water in long, thirsty swallows. "Sip; don't gulp!" Rosie reminds us. In outdoor skills we learned that gulping water could cause stomach cramps after a strenuous climb.

After lunch we do another group exploration, searching for something that will instruct us on what we are supposed to do next. I find a rock with words written on it in black marker: *white birch leaf.*

"That's it," says Rosie. "That's the kind of leaf we have to find." Taking the rock, she smiles at me, and suddenly I feel like a worthy and valuable member of the team. "Everyone hunt in this area where Louisa and I are standing," she instructs the group. "Search for rocks with words on them." She holds up my rock. "They look like this."

It seems I've found the right spot. As soon as the group gets to work, we uncover a treasure trove of printed stones, some large, some small. When we're done, we toss our rocks into a pile. "Now what?" asks Rae Gonzalez, from Erica Felstein's suite.

Rosie squats in front of the stones and turns different ones in her hands, examining them.

"Maybe if we put them together right, they'll make a message," Maddie suggests.

Rosie nods thoughtfully. "Maybe you're right," she agrees.

We instinctively break into groups of two and begin lining the rocks up in various configurations. It becomes like a giant game.

"Can we borrow the word *to* from you?"

"We almost have a sentence. Anyone got the word *tree*?"

"We have an extra rock with the word *water* written on it. Could anyone use it?"

The group works together with total cooperation. Mrs. Brewster and the staff had created the perfect team-building activity. At the end of an hour this is what we have:

Things you must find
White birch leaf
Water sample
One bug, identified
Moss sample, identified

Make camp at large boulder due south of present location. Find the face.

Calculate 36 hours from official end of Monday breakfast and return to cafeteria.

No one seems to know how to figure that last part out — anything that tells time was handed over on our first day, whether it was a phone, a notepad, or a watch.

Shielding her eyes, Rosie gazes at the sun. "Judging from the position of the sun, it's almost one o'clock in the afternoon," she figures.

"Evelyn, would you write this message down in your notebook so we don't forget anything?" Rosie requests.

"Okay," Evelyn agrees, but from the reluctant tone in her voice I can tell she doesn't like her secret notebook being mentioned so openly. Just the same, she takes the book out and writes down the message written in rocks on the ground.

After she's done, Evelyn and Rosie put their heads together — Rosie with the map, Evelyn with the compass — and they figure the best route due south. I don't know how we're ever going to find one boulder in a forest full of them. And what does *find the face* mean? When I ask that question, everyone looks to Rosie for the answer.

"No idea," Rosie admits. "I'm just hoping this face, whatever it is, will find us."

Fortunately, it does.

We hike back down into the dense forest once more. Descending isn't quite as difficult as going up, but it uses different muscles and I find my calves getting sore. It seems we're walking for a long time.

"Are you sure we're going the right way?" I ask, coming alongside Evelyn, who's checking her compass every few minutes.

"Of course I'm not sure," Evelyn answers.

I begin to think finding this boulder and this face is hopeless.

"I see it!" Maddie is the first to observe. "Right there." She points to a large, almost triangular boulder.

I laugh when I see that a sort of face is traced out in moss on the wide, flat northern surface of the boulder. It reminds me of the crater-formed face of the Man in the Moon.

144

"This is the spot. We'll make camp here," Rosie says.

We quickly see that someone from CMS has been here ahead of us. A large blue tarp covers a big black chest. Inside the chest are three .22-caliber rifles, the kind we've been practicing with, and three quivers loaded with arrows. There are also six two-person tents that are still collapsed and some pots and a pan for cooking.

Suddenly Erica Felstein gasps. "How come there's no food in there?" she asks Rosie.

Rosie surveys the rest of the area. "I guess we have to get it ourselves," she replies.

Erica throws her head back in despair. "I'm so tired and hungry! I can't find my own dinner! This is horrible!"

"Don't be such a baby," Rosie scolds her. "They gave us rifles and arrows. Obviously they expect us to catch our own meal."

"I wouldn't be able to catch anything even if I wanted to — and I *don't* want to," Erica insists. I'm annoyed by her whining, since it's already been a really long and tiring day. But on the other hand, I know exactly how she feels.

"Maybe we can find some berries and stuff," I suggest. "Remember, we learned about it."

Everyone nods enthusiastically when I say this. It seems no one feels good about shooting an animal for dinner.

We spend the next few hours hunting for some of the things on our list. We find the moss right away from the rock. One of the other girls in Anne's dorm is even able to identify it.

I slap a mosquito on my arm. "Here's our bug," I announce, dangling it by its wing.

Finding a white birch leaf among all these pines seems like it's going to be impossible until Maddie, Evelyn, and I come upon a gorgeous stand of birches. "Score!" Maddie cheers as she snaps off a leaf.

When we return to our campsite, six of the girls are busy setting up the two-person pup tents. Rosie and Anne have made a great fire. It crackles invitingly and the pleasant smell of burning pine permeates the campsite.

Maddie holds up the birch leaf for the group to see. "Excellent!" Rosie praises us as she takes a packet of tissues from her back pocket and lays the leaf between two sheets.

"Did you . . . uh . . . catch anything for supper?" I ask Rosie. I have such mixed feelings. Part of me hopes she hasn't. How gross to have to eat some cute little rabbit or a skinned squirrel! But another part of me — kind of a big part — would really like something to eat. I haven't had meat that wasn't made out of soy in a really long time.

"No. I tried," Rosie says. "The only animal I even saw was a squirrel running through the branches, and he was too fast for me. No one else would even attempt it, so I sent a crew out to see what they could forage."

It's evening now, and the dark pine needles overhead make it seem later than it probably really is. Four of our group return with the nylon bag. They take out a bunch of dandelion leaves, some wild blueberries, a good amount of dirty scallions, and some very small, underripe blackberries. "That's all you could find?" Rosie asks, displeased.

"We looked at some mushrooms but we weren't sure if they were good to eat or not," says a girl named Stacey.

"Well, it's better not to take a chance with mushrooms," Rosie agrees. She turns to Evelyn, Maddie, and me. "We could boil this into some kind of weak soup, I suppose. Do you think you guys can find water?"

"Sure," I say. "I heard the sound of running water back there when we were getting the birch leaf. We could probably follow the sound."

"Unless you think it's too *polluted*," Evelyn says pointedly to Rosie, unable to resist getting in a little dig.

"If we boil it, the water will probably be okay," Rosie replies.

So I pick up the largest of the pots and we set off in the dying light to find water. I try to remember what way we've come but it's harder than I would have thought. Everything looks pretty much the same.

"Do you know where we are?" Evelyn asks me. "Where did we see the creek?"

"I think it's a little farther this way," I say.

It's very quiet in the forest. The fallen pine needles have made a soft and fragrant carpet under our sneakers. Occasionally an animal snaps a small branch or a bird flits through the trees. We stop and I try to hear the sound of running water, but I can't.

Suddenly I'm aware of dark figures moving among the trees. Evelyn and Maddie notice them, too. We freeze, scared. Are there bears out here?

Whatever it is, there are two of them.

Should we run or just stay still?

A beam of vivid light suddenly cuts through the dusky gray. I see that Evelyn has a tiny flashlight built into her pen. In its light we can clearly see who these mysterious figures are. We are now face-to-face with two strangers.

Boys!

Chapter 12

"Our group leader sent us out to look for firewood," says Alonso, who's tall and thin with a head of thick, dark hair. He has large brown eyes that I'm horrified to find I can't stop staring at. It's been such a long time since I've seen a boy up close!

"We got so involved looking for the wood that we lost track of where we were," says the other boy, whose name is Ryan.

"You don't have any firewood," Maddie notes suspiciously. I have to give her credit for the observation — I hadn't even noticed. Of course, I'm in shock, being this close to real live boys.

"We dumped it when we realized we were lost. We've

been walking for a long time. I think we might be going in circles," Ryan says.

Ryan is Alonso's opposite, reddish blond, strongly built with bright blue eyes; also cute, just in a very different way.

"How can we even know if we're going in circles?" Alonso says, throwing his arms wide with frustration.

"It all looks the same out here," Ryan adds. "What I wouldn't give for a street sign right now!"

That makes me laugh. "I take it you're not a country boy," I say with a slight grin.

"No kidding!" Ryan cries, breaking into a smile. "I guess it shows."

"Kind of," Maddie agrees wryly.

Evelyn extends her palm and shows them the compass. "This will tell you if you're walking in circles or not."

"I *wish* we had a compass!" Alonso cries. "Our group leader, Joe, has one, but he's not sharing. How did you ever wrestle that away from yours?"

When he says this, I think of how Rosie has been designating different responsibilities to different team members. Although she's bossy, she doesn't hog everything for herself. I make a note to remind Maddie of this later.

"This is actually mine," Evelyn says. "I brought it with me. I'd lend it to you but I don't know how I'd ever get it back."

"I know," Ryan says. "They keep us separated like something awful will happen if we got together. One cool girl waved to us one time and the headmaster had a conniption."

"That was me!" I say.

"For real?" Ryan asks, delighted.

"Yeah, for real!"

Ryan raises his hand and I slap him five. "That was so cool — and then all the other girls started waving."

"We noticed you might be getting in trouble because of it."

"Yeah, we got scolded. But who cares?" Ryan answers. "It was worth it to know there were actual girls nearby. This place is so weird. I've been going to school with girls since kindergarten."

"Are the three of you lost, too?" Alonso asks.

"No. Compass. Remember?" Evelyn answers. "We just came down for some water. We'll be boiling a hearty berry and grass soup for supper. Yummy!"

"Berries and grass?" Alonso lets out a bark of laughter. "You're kidding, right?"

"I wish I was," Evelyn tells him. "We're all so hungry! But that's all we could find to eat."

Alonso digs in his backpack and pulls out several wax-paper packages of potato chips. Instantly, my mouth begins to water. "Here, you guys can have these," he offers.

Ryan offers more bags of chips and two apples. "I also have some sandwiches in here that are left over from our lunch. Your group can have them."

"We can't take your food," Maddie protests, though her eyes are wide with longing, too. "What will you eat?"

"We brought in lots of food," Alonso tells us. "If we ever find our way back to our campsite, we could give you more."

"You didn't happen to see a creek in your travels, did you?" I ask. "I know it's around here somewhere."

"It's right behind where we just came from," Alonso says. "Come on. We'll show you."

They take us directly to the creek and we fill the pot with water that looks cool and fresh. "There's nothing wrong with this water," Evelyn says as we scoop it into the pot with the cups from our mess kits. "Rosie is just buying into all the lies they're feeding us at Country Manor."

"What lies?" Alonso asks.

"Our headmistress says the lake is polluted," Maddie explains.

"We were just swimming in it," Ryan says.

"See?" Evelyn remarks knowingly.

"What other lies?" Alonso asks, seeming keen to know.

"I'm not sure, but something is definitely going on at CMS," Evelyn tells him. She's in her conspiracy-theory element and finally has a new audience. "Why did they have to take all our electronic devices? If they don't work, just let us hang on to them. And why the big secrecy about where we are? Who's really going to want to come hurt us? We're just a bunch of teenagers."

"I agree with you," Alonso says. "Things have seemed dicey to me right from the start."

"Paranoid much?" I crack, trying to get along, but frankly sick of Evelyn's constant worries.

"Maybe, maybe not," Maddie says.

"So, if you're not a country boy, where *are* you from?" I ask Ryan. He's helping me carry the pot of water, which is really heavy now that it's full. We've fallen behind the rest of the group, trying to not spill any water, and I'm happy to have a chance to talk to him.

"Chicago."

"Chicago!" I cry happily. "Me, too!"

"Wow!" Ryan says. "Cool! What do you miss most about it?"

"Not a thing," I reply. "It's crowded and dirty and my parents don't let me out of their sights for a minute. What's to miss?"

155

"It wasn't always like that," Ryan says.

He makes me think of the wide streets, beautiful stores, the theaters and restaurants. The lake. The fountain. "I know," I agree sadly. "But that's not how it is now. Besides, I love CMS."

"I do, too, but I miss the Field Museum; at least, the parts that are still open," Ryan says.

"Yeah," I agree. The second time the river flooded, the gorgeous museum of natural history and science was practically destroyed. It was a horrible disaster. It was on a day when the museum was closed so no one was hurt, but it ruined big parts of the museum. Priceless, irreplaceable artifacts like rare fossils and skeletons of extinct animals were destroyed forever.

"Even though it's a wreck, I loved going there," Ryan says wistfully.

"My favorite was the Art Institute," I remember fondly. "Before the fire, of course." It hurts to even think about it. It was in the first year of the War and the Alliance claimed responsibility for igniting a fire that scorched through all the exhibition hallways. Everything was destroyed. I couldn't stand to think of my favorites, the French Impressionists like Monet and Seurat, all those great paintings charred beyond recognition.

The memory of it made me want to change the subject.

"You love CMS, too? What do you like most about it?" I ask.

"The athletic program," Ryan replies. "There was nothing at my old school. Here it feels so good to move. They really challenge you, too. I've done stuff I never thought I could do."

"Like what?"

"I just learned to swim. Never ever swam before. And it turns out I'm good at it."

"I can't believe it!" I cry. "I *love* to swim. They have the best pool in the world in our gym, though I haven't gotten to really swim in it yet. So far all we've done is canoe. But that's something I'd never done before."

"Exactly!" Ryan says. "There are all these new things! I'm learning so much. CMS is awesome."

"What do you think of Evelyn's theories?"

"Alonso is just like her," Ryan tells me. "He's a great guy but I think his imagination has gone too wild. It could be that CMS is so cool that it seems too good to be true — so he thinks it can't be, you know?"

"Makes sense." It's a smart conclusion, I think.

As we get closer to our campsite, I can see that Maddie, Evelyn, and Alonso are talking to Rosie. Rosie doesn't look too happy. In fact, her arms fly up into the air in an angry gesture. She's shouting at them.

"That doesn't look good," I mutter.

"No," Ryan agrees, looking worried. "It doesn't."

As we get even closer, I start to hear what Rosie is shouting.

"Have you missed the point of this weekend completely? We can't just count on running into other people with food. It's all about taking care of *ourselves*!"

"But we *did* run into people who are willing to give us food," Maddie protests. "So we had a break; so what?"

"This is stupid!" Evelyn shouts back at Rosie. "I've been walking all day and I'm hungry. Starving! And they have food. I want to eat!"

"Then pick up a rifle and shoot something!" Rosie shouts back.

All the other girls have stopped what they were doing and are watching the argument.

"You're the best shooter in the group, and you couldn't hit anything," Maddie reminds Rosie.

"I'm pretty good with a rifle," Alonso offers. "I could give it a try if you'd like."

"Nooooo!" Rosie wails. "All of you are *so* not getting it!"

I need to smooth this over somehow. I pick up our pace, closing the last yards between us and the campsite, and Ryan hurries to keep up. "I have the water!" I call out when we've just about reached them.

"Great, but you were supposed to carry it yourself," Rosie snaps.

We set down the bucket and I decide to ignore the criticism. "Rosie, this is Ryan. Ryan, Rosie. And I guess you've met Alonso."

"I don't care who they are!" she shouts. "Contact with the boys is totally forbidden. They're not even supposed to *be* here." She gestures toward the others in our group. "One of them is bound to slip up and say something. Then we'll all be in trouble."

There's a murmur of discontent from the others. "Can we just have the sandwiches?" Anne Abadi asks, though it's more a command than a request. "We're all really starving."

Anne's words are echoed by the other girls. Rosie turns toward them and seems to realize an uprising is brewing. "Do what you want," she huffs at the group, and she stomps over to her tent. "I don't care anymore."

When Rosie disappears into her tent, we all just stand there for a minute, silently looking at one another.

"Do you want the sandwiches or not?" Alonso finally asks, speaking to Maddie and Evelyn. They look to me for an opinion.

"Sure. Why not?" I say with a shrug. I look to the others. "Here's the water if anyone is thirsty or would rather make soup."

Everyone's thirsty. No one wants the soup.

We all eat, including Ryan and Alonso. Maddie, Evelyn, and I sit down with them.

"So, Alonso, I know Ryan is from Chicago like we are. Where are you from?" I ask.

"Nowhere," Alonso says, looking out into the forest.

Maddie laughs lightly. "You must be from somewhere," she insists. "Everyone's from someplace."

"Out east," Alonso says. "I've moved around a lot. Here and there. You know."

I get the feeling he doesn't want to talk about his home. But that's okay; we have more important matters to discuss. "If you guys had a compass, could you find your way back to your group?" I ask.

Alonso and Ryan nod as they chew their sandwiches.

Our map is tucked into the top of Rosie's half-open backpack, which is still propped against a log outside her tent. I get up and slide it out. "Evelyn, could you get us back to school without the compass?" I ask.

"Definitely not," Evelyn answers. "But I have my own, remember?" Reaching into her pocket, she hands Alonso her compass.

"Are you sure?" Alonso asks as she hands it over.

"Absolutely," Evelyn says. "You'd better get going. You don't have much light left. There's a small flashlight built into it. Just press." She demonstrates and shoots a small beam around the campsite.

Suddenly I realize how dark it really is. The other girls are all heading into their tents to sleep. "If you don't get back, will your group search for you?" I ask the boys.

"They might. We'd better go," Ryan says, getting up. "Thanks for your help."

"Thanks for the food," Maddie says.

Alonso stands by the fire and studies the compass by the flickering light from the dying flames. He turns in the direction we came from. "Okay. I think I know what to do," he murmurs. Together, he and Ryan pick up their backpacks and head out.

Maddie yawns and stretches. "I have to sleep."

"Me, too," Evelyn agrees. With a wave, Maddie crawls into the tent she's sharing with Evelyn.

"See ya bright and early for more fun and games in

the great outdoors," Evelyn says wryly as she also heads for the tent.

Suddenly I'm hit with the overwhelming fatigue they're feeling. But I have a problem. I'm sharing a tent with Rosie, and I'm sort of dreading getting in there with her. If she wakes up — or isn't even asleep yet — it's going to be tense, to say the least.

Gazing up at the sky, I see twinkling stars spinning off into a field of clear, dark navy blue. The brilliant three-quarter moon lights up everything. A beautiful night, the clearest I've seen in I don't know how many years.

Luckily, my sleeping bag is still rolled and lashed to the bottom of my backpack. I know my ground cloth is rolled into it and will keep away any dampness.

In an instant, I'm up and untying the sleeping roll from my pack. I'm so tired that I'd rather sleep out here than risk facing Rosie's anger inside our tent. Finding a flat spot covered with pine needles, I spread out my things and crawl inside the sleeping bag. In about a second, I'm asleep.

Maybe I slept a long time before I started to dream. It could be that I had other dreams that I can't recall. But what I remember is this: Maddie, Evelyn, Rosie, and I are captured in a dark and sinister castle. Mrs. Brewster is there sweeping the floor, using an old broom with a branch for a handle. Every time she looks up at us she cackles a witch's frightening laugh. There's a crystal ball on the table, and suddenly a picture appears in it. It's my parents. I run to the ball and see them home in Chicago. Mom's sick in bed. I have to get home to her. "Mom! Dad!" I shout, but they can't hear me.

My eyes snap open and I sit up in my sleeping bag.

Everything is pink and bluish gray. I'm not sure where I am for a second. Smelling the charred embers of last night's fire helps me to remember. But something's not right. I know this for sure, though at first I can't make sense of it.

I wake up just a little more and it hits me.

"Evelyn! Maddie!" I shout. "Get up!"

They scramble out of the tent and look around. Their faces are as confused and upset as mine must be.

We're alone. The rest of the campsite has been cleared away.

Chapter 13

1 can't believe they left us!" Maddie cries. "They must have gotten up before dawn and gone."

"But why?" Evelyn wonders out loud.

"Rosie," Maddie says. "She somehow convinced the others to leave us behind."

The moment Maddie says this, I know she's right. She probably told them we were going to get into trouble for bringing the boys, so they should separate themselves from us. She could have said a lot of things: that we didn't want to leave with them; that we had a different assignment and would catch up later. She might have said anything.

I'm so frustrated and disappointed I want to cry.

"Let's not freak out," Evelyn says. "They can't have left too much earlier. It's just getting light now. I have the compass, so we can find our way down. We might even get back to school before they do. I don't know how they'll manage without a compass."

Evelyn rummages in her backpack. "I know it's in here," she murmurs. Her digging becomes more and more frantic.

"What's the matter?" I ask her.

"The compass," Evelyn says. "It's gone. Rosie must have taken it with her."

"So how do we get back?" Maddie asks.

"I don't know," Evelyn admits. "I have no idea."

Fifteen minutes later we've packed up Maddie and Evelyn's tent and we're looking out into the woods, our backpacks over our shoulders, with absolutely no idea where to go.

I am so unbelievably angry at Rosie. How could she have done this to us? My stomach grumbles with fierce hunger. Not only am I starving but my muscles ache from sleeping on the ground last night. There was some kind of rock under my shoulder that my sleeping bag couldn't cushion me from.

I wish I was anywhere but here.

"When we were heading north, we were climbing up. So going down will be south," Evelyn says. "I think it's southeast, actually."

"The sun rises in the east and sets in the west, right?" I say, not sure I'm remembering correctly.

"That's right, but we can't see the sun under these pines," Maddie points out.

"True," I agree.

"Here goes nothing," says Evelyn as she steps into the forest.

We follow her, not talking. I don't know how we'll ever make it back to CMS. It's just trees and more trees. There's nothing to follow, not even a path.

The idea of getting lost in the woods suddenly seems like a very real possibility, and it terrifies me. We have no food and one tent between the three of us. "Listen for the creek," I suggest after a while. "Maybe we can figure our way from there. At least we'll always have water."

"Look! Look! Look!" Maddie cries excitedly, pointing.

Two people are walking in the woods ahead of us. Alonso and Ryan!

"Guys!" I shout, waving my arm in wide arcs. "Over here! It's us!"

They wave back and hurry toward us. We crash through the bushes to meet up with them. "Have you been walking all night?" Evelyn asks.

"No," Alonso says. "It got pitch-black. Even with this little flashlight we couldn't see where we were going. So we just slept by a rock."

"You don't even have sleeping bags," Maddie says.

"Tell me about it," Ryan says, stretching his back. "And it was cold, too."

"Do you still have the compass I gave you?" Evelyn asks.

Ryan and Alonso nod and show her. "We're following it down now. Want to hike together?"

"Sure we do," Maddie agrees. "We're totally lost."

"Where's the rest of your group?" Ryan asks.

We begin to walk as we tell them how our group ditched us. "Did they do that because of us?" Ryan asks.

"I'm pretty sure, yeah," I answer. "Rosie can't stand the idea that we might get into trouble for taking your food. I think she's nuts, though. You guys were lost. Should we have just walked away and left you stranded in the forest? I don't think that would be the right thing to do, would it?"

"Totally not," Ryan says.

"If Rosie gets there first, I wonder what she'll say to Mrs. Brewster," Evelyn worries. "What explanation will she give for us not being with the group?"

This has been worrying me, too. "Maybe she'll wait for us before going into the cafeteria," I suggest. Despite the way she acted last night, I just can't believe that Rosie would completely betray us. Still, the evidence isn't in her favor. After all, she's left us to get lost in the woods.

Or has she?

"Hey, everybody," I alert them. "Check this out." I squat to observe an interesting pile of stones stacked at the base of a tree. A small brown feather is stuck between the top two stones.

"Is it a cairn?" Maddie asks as she bends to look at the pile.

"It's a rock trail marker, all right," Ryan says. "That feather tells us it's not a natural formation."

Nodding, I smile, knowing Rosie left it for us. She might have intended to leave us on our own, but regretted it once they got going and it was too late to turn back. Or maybe she intended to mark the trail all along. She just wanted to get back at us for the Alonso and Ryan thing.

"I wonder how far apart these are set," Alonso considers. He checks Evelyn's compass and waves us on.

My stomach rumbles. We've shared the last two sandwiches that were left over from the night before. It wasn't really enough, but it was better than nothing. Ryan hears the sound and turns to me. "We each had our last bag of chips this morning," he says. "Sorry; nothing's left."

"Keep an eye out for berries, I guess," Maddie says.

"I love berries," Ryan says. "I love them on top of a great apple cobbler," he adds.

"Don't talk like that," Evelyn pleads. "I don't want to think about food."

We've been walking only about ten minutes when we reach the next cairn.

"Good," says Alonso. "We're going the right way. Everybody watch for signs that other people have walked through here. You know, footprints, broken branches, stuff like that."

Looking down, I see a mark in the dirt. "Sneaker print," I announce.

"Cool," says Evelyn, "let's keep going."

We hurry on until we can see the CMS buildings through the trees. They're still in the distance, but they're there. I'm flooded with relief at the sight of them.

"Almost home," Ryan says.

"If you want to call CMS home," Maddie says sourly.

"Right now it's home enough to me," Ryan replies.

I'm happy he says it so I don't have to. I agree absolutely. I'm so happy to see it.

"We have to get around the lake, but you guys can just go straight ahead," Alonso says. "I even see another cairn right down there."

We look and see it, too. Our way back is all laid out.

Alonso hands Evelyn her compass back. She reaches for it but then hesitates. "Can you find your way back without it?" she asks.

"Yeah, this path is easy," Ryan states confidently. "We come this way all the time."

"You do?" I ask. "I thought it was forbidden."

"It is, but so what?" Ryan says with a laugh.

"Why do you risk it?" I ask.

"Just to look around, see what's going on over here," Ryan says. "It's mostly the fun of sneaking out and getting back in without being caught."

Evelyn takes the compass from Alonso. "We'd better get back," she says. "We might be able to catch up with our group if we hurry."

"Good luck," Ryan says as he and Alonso walk away.

We wave and head toward the next cairn. "Is anyone else besides me nervous about what might happen when we go back?" Maddie asks.

"No. Nothing's going to happen," I say, sounding confident and upbeat. But I'm totally lying. I'm as nervous as she is. Maybe even more.

We arrive at the door to the cafeteria just as Rosie is coming out. "Oh, look who showed up," she says nastily, looking at Evelyn, Maddie, and me with distaste.

"Did you accomplish your special mission?" Carole Osterly asks as she walks out behind Rosie.

Studying her, I try to decide if she's being sarcastic, but quickly realize she's asking this question in all innocence. She truly thinks we were on some kind of mission.

"What special mission?" Maddie asks.

"The one where you were supposed to follow trail markers down," Carole says. She turns to Rosie. "Isn't that what you told us?" she checks.

"Yeah. I guess they made it because they're here," Rosie replies with no warmth at all. "Score one for our team."

Now I'm really confused. Was this really a test or did Rosie leave us behind out of spite? Evelyn and Maddie are just as bewildered. I can tell from their expressions.

"I guess we did," I say to Carole. "Who laid the cairns?"

"Rosie," Carole answers.

"You made better time than I thought you would," Rosie says.

We had a little help from compass-carrying friends, I think, but don't say it. Let her believe we managed on our own.

"We have the rest of Sunday free," Carole tells us as she heads down the path. "I can't wait to get into the shower. Then I'm going to sleep right through to tomorrow morning."

"That sounds wonderful," Evelyn agrees.

Rosie sees her friend Mary and walks toward her without even a wave to us. Maddie hisses an insult under her breath, but Rosie doesn't seem to hear it. "I can't stand her," she says, more loudly this time.

Rosie never comes up to the suite as the three of us unpack and clean up. After showering, Evelyn disappears into her room. Maddie has already fallen asleep in our room, waiting for Evelyn to come out of the shower. She's on her top bunk, still wrapped in her bathrobe.

I figure it's better to let her sleep.

On my way to the shower, I stop by one of our tall windows and peer out through the bars. Rosie is playing soccer on the lawn with the same group of athletes she's been friends with from the beginning.

Seeing her there — and knowing that she's purposely avoiding being in our room — makes me feel emotions I can't really identify. What is it exactly that I'm feeling?

I'm angry at her, for sure. Even if she didn't intend to leave us lost in the woods, she was happy enough to let us believe we were lost. What was her point? Was it that if we didn't obey her, she'd take strong revenge, that she'd make us pay for it? What kind of friend does that?

At the same time, though, I'm sad to lose what little ground I'd gained with Rosie in the last two weeks. I was really getting to like her. In some ways, being around her was so easy — I could just be myself. I didn't have to worry about CMS, like I do with Evelyn. And I didn't have to be strong or defensive, like I always feel with Maddie lately.

Evelyn comes out of her room still wrapped in her white terry robe. "I leaned against the wall in the shower and almost fell asleep standing up," she says.

"Rosie's playing soccer with her friends down there," I report, nodding toward the window.

"She's nuts," Evelyn says with a dismissive wave toward the window. "I'm setting my alarm for dinnertime and I'm sleeping until then."

"Good idea," I say as I head in to take my shower. "Wake me and Maddie up when it rings."

"Will do," Evelyn agrees with a yawn.

The shower spray is so wonderful on my achy back and shoulders. Just like Evelyn, I find my eyes sliding shut before I rally and shake myself awake again. Drying off, I wrap myself in a towel and trudge back to my bedroom, where I pull on my nightshirt and collapse into bed. There are no dreams of crystal balls now. Just the dark, infinite tunnel of bottomless, exhausted sleep.

• • •

When I open my eyes, the light coming through the bedroom window is muted, dusky. I glance to my dresser, where the digital readout on my battery-powered clock tells me that I have ten minutes to get to the cafeteria for supper.

Instantly, I am up and shaking Maddie, who's snoring on her top bunk. "We're going to miss dinner," I say as her eyelids flutter open.

In a second she is fully awake. "Oh, no, we're not," she insists, throwing off her blanket. "I'm not going to bed hungry two nights in a row."

I've never seen her dress so fast. "Hurry," she urges me as I tie my sneaker laces.

Before leaving the dorm, I go across to Evelyn's bedroom to check that she hasn't overslept. I knock loudly, but I get no answer.

"I asked Evelyn to wake us," I complain. "I guess she went ahead."

"She must have forgotten," Maddie says.

"I suppose so," I agree, trying not to be too annoyed. Everyone makes mistakes, I remind myself.

When we reach the cafeteria, Maddie and I get our food and sit down together. Rosie is with her sporty friends and doesn't even glance at us.

"Rosie's not sitting with us anymore," I note as I lift a forkful of rigatoni with tomato sauce to my lips.

"Who cares?" says Maddie, who is completely involved in her macaroni and cheese.

"Do you see Evelyn?" I ask, scanning the cafeteria for her.

"Nuh-uh," Maddie answers. She puts down her fork and cranes her neck around to see all the tables. "Strange," she says.

"It is," I agree. "Maybe she's in the bathroom." As we eat, I keep watching for Evelyn, but she never appears.

Emmanuelle approaches our table. "Madeleine Ballinger?" she checks, looking at Maddie. Maddie doesn't have as many classes with Emmanuelle as I do.

I nudge Maddie's leg under the table.

"Yes, that's me," Maddie says.

"And Louisa, Mrs. Brewster would like to see the two of you in her office after you're finished eating."

A knot forms in the pit of my stomach. "Do you know why?" I ask with an unexpected scratchiness in my voice. I suddenly feel sure Rosie has turned us in for our supposed misbehavior on the overnight.

Emmanuelle doesn't answer my question. "Just finish your meals and go to the office," she says.

Under the table, Maddie grabs my wrist nervously. I'm sure she's had the same thought about Rosie.

"We'll be right there," I manage to tell Emmanuelle, although I'm so full of anxiety that I have to choke out the words.

"Yes, right away," Maddie adds as she gets up and goes to return her tray. We weren't really done eating, but we're definitely not hungry anymore.

What if Mrs. Brewster decides to send us home? I would hate that so much. Of course, Maddie wouldn't mind. She might even be glad. Evelyn might be happy about it, too.

Thinking of Evelyn makes me glance around the cafeteria once more, searching for her.

Where *is* she?

Chapter 14

The first thing I notice when Maddie and I arrive at Mrs. Brewster's high-ceilinged office with its bank of tall windows is that Evelyn is not there, either. I'd hoped she'd also been summoned here since she was part of our group. I'm starting to really get worried about her.

Mrs. Brewster sits behind her big wooden desk and she is not smiling. My mind shifts from Evelyn and begins to race a mile a minute, practicing different ways to smooth this over.

We couldn't just leave the boys lost and alone in the woods. What if they had died?

It was for the good of our team. We found something to eat, didn't we?

We were demonstrating adaptability and resourcefulness. Those are two qualities that our outdoor skills teacher always stresses.

It seems to me that all the arguments I'm about to make are true and valid.

"Sit, please," Mrs. Brewster requests, nodding toward two low, straight-backed chairs across from her desk.

I sit, my shoulders back, alert and ready to make my points.

Cutting my eyes to Maddie, I notice that her right leg is jiggling anxiously. I'm surprised — and just a little happy — to see this. I figure it means she *doesn't* want to be sent home. If she wants to stay, she'll put out the effort required to convince Mrs. Brewster that neither of us did anything wrong.

"Mrs. Brewster, this was really not our fault," I begin.

"Did I give you permission to speak, Ms. Ballinger?" Mrs. Brewster questions coldly.

"No, ma'am," I admit.

"Then do not speak," Mrs. Brewster says.

"Yes, ma'am."

Admittedly, not a great start.

Moments of silence pass. Are we waiting for Evelyn? We must be.

"I'm sure Evelyn will be here any minute," I say impulsively, forgetting about the whole do-not-speak thing in my panic.

Mrs. Brewster's eyebrows shoot up and her nostrils flare. Her blue eyes burn into me.

"Sorry, sorry," I say, realizing my error. "Sorry."

Another few minutes pass and finally the office door opens. But Devi, not Evelyn, enters. She holds a stack of papers that she places on the desk in front of Mrs. Brewster.

Suddenly a new worry takes hold of me. What if this is *about* Evelyn? Has something awful happened to her?

"Ms. Ballinger, Madeleine," Mrs. Brewster begins, "Devi has been reviewing the identity bracelets we collected and she informs me that yours doesn't check out."

My throat is instantly dry as sandpaper. By the end of the first week I'd assumed we were safe on that score. I'd almost forgotten all about it.

"Really? That's odd," Maddie bluffs like a champ. "What's the problem?"

I'm astounded by her coolness, and I hope my astonishment doesn't show.

Mrs. Brewster leans forward, her elbows on her desk, her hands locked together. "When we scan your ID bracelet, two numbers come up. One code set traces to Madeleine Ballinger and then a second code comes up with different numbers that belong to a Madeleine Frye. Do you know anyone by that name?"

Maddie shakes her head. She turns to me. "We don't know anybody named Frye, do we, sis?"

I'd never have guessed she was capable of this kind of calm deceit. If they still gave out Academy Awards for acting, Maddie would win one. And she's never called me *sis* before, but it sounds totally natural.

"No, I can't think of anyone with that name." I'm grateful my voice doesn't crack and hope my acting is even half as good as hers is.

Maddie turns back to Mrs. Brewster and Devi. Her face is all wide-eyed innocence as she shrugs.

I feel like I might vomit.

Mrs. Brewster's eyes narrow and seem to somehow grow brighter. They dart between Maddie and me. She's sizing us up suspiciously, taking our measure, deciding if we're lying.

I think about swimming — anything to keep my face calm and neutral. I see myself in a pool, looking down through the aqua water to the cool blue-tiled bottom. I am breathing in and breathing out. Breathing in. Breathing out.

"Devi, take Ms. Madeleine Ballinger or Frye, whichever it is, to the isolation quarters, please," Mrs. Brewster instructs.

Maddie looks at me and, for the first time, panic flashes in her eyes. I hope Mrs. Brewster hasn't glimpsed it.

Maddie must sense that she's possibly given herself away, because she ducks her head down. A quick moment later when she lifts it again, she's cool once more. "Do I really have to go to these other quarters?" she asks. "I've never slept away from my sister before and the thought of it really scares me."

Nice save, Maddie, I think with deep admiration.

"It's true," I say. "Never apart. I won't sleep at all tonight if she's not there."

Mrs. Brewster shakes her head firmly. "I can't give the two of you the opportunity to coordinate your story."

"What story!?" Maddie asks with convincing indignation.

"If you're telling a story," Devi allows in a more kindly tone.

"We're not," I insist. "We don't know how this happened. It's not our fault."

Mrs. Brewster looks at me sharply. "What did you think this was about when you first came in, Ms. Ballinger?" she asks pointedly.

I'm angry at myself for using the sentence *It's not our fault* a second time. I know it's what's reminded her of when I said it earlier.

I hope I can be as cool and quick as Maddie has been, but I know I can't come up with a lie that fast. So I stick with the facts.

"We met some boys while on the overnight and accepted some sandwiches from them. They'd gotten lost. We helped them find their way back. I know we're not supposed to have contact with them, but it seemed like the right thing to do at the time." I'm gambling that by admitting the truth, I'll come across as honest.

To my total amazement, Mrs. Brewster smiles.

I've never seen her do this. Honestly, it doesn't look natural on her. It's actually a little scary.

"Life throws unexpected things at us," the head-mistress says. "Adaptability and ingenuity are key."

"Yes," I agree cautiously. "Emmanuelle always tells us that."

"I taught it to her." Mrs. Brewster then resumes her former stern expression. "You ladies will have to adjust to being apart tonight. That is all. Dismissed."

Now Maddie is unable to conceal the alarm on her face as Devi takes her arm and hurries her out of the room. Mrs. Brewster waits for me at the door and, once I am in the hall, takes her keys and locks it. "Straight to your room, Ms. Ballinger. It's almost seven thirty." With that, she heads away from me, moving down the hall at a brisk clip.

I'm left standing there alone, hardly believing what's happened. I let everything rewind in my head, reviewing what was said, trying to make sense of it.

The guy Mom and Dad hired to alter Maddie's bracelet hadn't done the job correctly. A shadow of her old code was still there.

If CMS uncovered the truth, then I would be in trouble, too. I've been claiming Maddie as my twin sister all this time.

Maddie would be sent home and so would I.

Chapter 15

Not knowing what else to do, I hurry back toward my room. What a disaster this day has been!

First Rosie and . . . everything.

Then Evelyn goes missing.

Now Maddie is being held like a prisoner in some isolation quarters. I discover that being torn from my best friend — who really has become more like a sister, right down to how annoying she can be sometimes — is the most devastating loss of all.

I enter our dorm, desperately needing someone to talk to. "Is Evelyn here?" I ask Rosie, whom I find sitting at the table, reading by lamplight.

"How would I know?" Rosie answers in a flat voice, not even glancing up from her book.

I head straight for my room and find my locket in my top drawer. Clicking it open, I gaze down at the photos of my parents. "Mom, Dad? What should I do?" I whisper. "We're in big trouble and I wish I could talk to you about it." Closing it, I put the locket around my neck and hold it against my heart. Just for tonight, I need to wear it.

"Talking to yourself again?" Rosie snipes when I return to the living room.

Her cold tone is just the last straw. I'm unable to stand her icy disregard anymore. It's more than I can take. Feeling overwhelmed, I collapse to my knees in tears.

Rosie looks up from her homework in alarm and is immediately at my side. "Louisa, what is it? What's happened?"

"It's Maddie . . . She . . . We . . ." My voice trails off. I have a dilemma now. How much should I tell Rosie? Why should I trust her? Is it even safe to confide in her?

I felt so close to her this last week, but she's betrayed our new friendship. Or has she? Is this just a disagreement that will blow over? Is it really the huge rift it seems to be right now?

Deciding I can't take the chance, I choose not to divulge the whole story. "There's something wrong with her bracelet," I say, opting for a half-truth. "They don't believe us that it's a mistake and Mrs. Brewster put Maddie in some isolation quarters somewhere."

"What kind of something wrong?" Rosie asks.

"Her bracelet says she's someone else."

"Because she *is* someone else," Rosie states evenly.

Looking up sharply, my jaw drops in shock at her words. I search her face. Is she testing me, or does she know this for sure? "Why do you say that?" I ask.

"She's not a thing like you. And you most certainly are not twins, fraternal or otherwise."

"Fraternal twins are more like sisters than twins," I argue.

"You don't have the body language of sisters, especially not sisters so close in age," Rosie insists calmly.

"Sisters melt into each other; they sit back to back, shoulder to shoulder. They borrow each other's clothing without asking. You and Maddie are super close — anyone can see that — but not sisters."

Should I insist that she's wrong? Somehow I just don't want to lie to her anymore. And, anyway, she's already figured it out. "You're right," I admit. "It was a trick to get Maddie into the school. We weren't hurting anyone."

I am surprised — and relieved — when Rosie wraps me in a hug. Our feud is instantly forgotten.

"Now we have to figure out what to do," Rosie says as she releases me from her embrace.

"We could just do nothing," I suggest. "This could just blow over. Mrs. Brewster might forget about it."

"No," Rosie disagrees, shaking her head. "I don't think Mrs. Brewster is a *forget about it* kind of person."

Sighing, I know she's right. We sit in silence, each trying to come up with a plan and failing.

The scratch of a key turning in the door makes us both jump. But to my relief, Evelyn walks in, waving a flashlight around the dimly lit room.

191

"Where have you been?!" I cry, getting to my feet.

"Making lights-out checks," she replies, as if I should have known this.

"All this time?" I question.

A sheepish, secretive expression crosses her face.

"You weren't here before dinner," I add. "And you didn't wake me up like you promised."

Evelyn snaps her fingers. "Sorry about that. I knew there was something I forgot. I just got involved in . . . what I was doing."

"Which was?" Rosie prompts.

Evelyn steps in closer to us and lowers her voice. "Investigating."

"Investigating what?" The note of irritation that always creeps into Rosie's voice when Evelyn's on the conspiracy warpath is loud and clear.

Evelyn dangles a set of keys. "I scored these from the patrol office. There's no door I can't get into. But I have to return them before anyone notices they're gone."

Rosie's jaw drops. "You're crazy! You have to put those back right now!" she says, her voice suddenly dropping to a frantic whisper. "Do you know what kind of trouble you'll get into if you're caught?"

"I won't," Evelyn promises. "First tell me why you two look so upset. What's happened?"

We fill her in on the whole story. "We don't know what to do about it," I moan.

"And your 'investigating' isn't going to help!" Rosie adds angrily. "We're already in trouble!"

"Why don't we go have a look around," Evelyn suggests, once more holding up her keys.

"Right now?" I ask.

"It's now or never," Evelyn replies. "Who knows when I'll be able to get my hands on these again?"

Evelyn hands out certain keys to Rosie and me so that we, too, can sneak into the main building. We look at each other, dubious about this plan. But Evelyn says she knows where they're probably holding Maddie — she's seen a room marked DISCIPLINE in the basement of the main hall.

"What were you doing in the basement of the main hall?" Rosie asks, shocked.

"Investigating, obviously!" Evelyn says indignantly.

Rosie huffs. "What could you possibly be investigating?"

"I want to know what the real deal is on this crazy school," Evelyn insists. "You two can think CMS is a slice of heaven, but something *weird* is going on here."

"Like what, exactly?" Rosie counters. "You've been saying it's weird here for weeks, but everything seems just fine to the rest of us!"

"Like what school wants you to survive in the forest with no food packed? Who *does* that?" Evelyn argues. "Tell me that's not more than a little weird."

"It's a life skill," Rosie insists.

"It's not a skill I would need if they didn't make us go out into the woods overnight!" Evelyn replies.

"Let's go find Maddie, already!" I cry, fed up with their squabbling.

"I can't come with you. I have to finish my rounds," Evelyn says. "You guys better go right now, though, because these keys need to be back by the end of my shift."

"Okay," I agree.

"Let's go," Rosie says.

With a satisfying click, the dead-bolt lock on the back door of the main building opens. The door creaks ever so slightly when I push it open, but to me the sound might as well be thunder. My skin crawls with gooseflesh and my heart pounds.

"This is insane," Rosie whispers as she follows me into the dark hallway.

I nod in agreement, but it doesn't stop me from moving farther into the hall. Each of us still has a small flashlight from our camping trip. We switch them on and create a circle of soft light around us.

The building is mostly silent with the kind of big, overwhelming quiet that can be unnerving. Every once in a while, though, a pipe bangs as the water heater turns on, or the building makes a creaky settling noise. When that happens, Rosie and I jump. It's hard to not freak out at every little thing.

"How do we get to the basement?" Rosie asks in a whisper.

I have no idea. We don't have very specific instructions. Back in the dorm room I was distracted by my own panic and Evelyn and Rosie's fighting. It made me forget to ask Evelyn to draw us a map.

"Maybe we should split up and look for it separately," I suggest. "We can meet again by the back door in, say, about a half hour."

"Okay," Rosie agrees. "I'll go to the end of this hallway and see if I can find a stairway down."

As Rosie becomes a receding spot of light in the darkness, I scan my flashlight around. A turn in the hall is revealed in the illumination and I follow it around a corner.

At once, I freeze. I hear something — noises. Voices!

Barely daring to breathe, I follow the sounds. They bring me two doors down. I put my ear to the door.

Something's not right. There seem to be more people speaking than could fit into one of these classroom-sized rooms.

Flashing lights are coming from under the door. Where have I seen that kind of light before? It's very familiar.

And all of a sudden I know what it is.

A television!

How can this be? I thought television and radio waves didn't reach us here at CMS.

Wait until I tell Evelyn this!

Mrs. Brewster is in there. I recognize her voice. She's speaking to other people. I hear Devi and also Emmanuelle. And some of the other teachers. I wonder if it's a meeting of all our teachers.

I know I should get out of there, but my curiosity wins out over my better judgment. Getting to the floor, I lie flat so I can hear the voices more clearly through the door's bottom opening.

"Quiet, everyone," Mrs. Brewster is saying. "The president is about to speak."

The room grows silent, except for the sound of the television. I'm aware of my own heartbeat as I wait with the others to hear what he will say. Something tells me some important event has occurred in the outside world — something really significant.

"Ladies and gentlemen," the president begins. "It is my sad duty to inform you that at ten o'clock this morning, Canada surrendered to the Alliance."

Completely shocked, I clap my hand over the stunned gasp that almost escaped my lips. Canada has been a United States ally throughout the War. No one ever seriously thought the Alliance could infiltrate Canada, let alone take it over. This is terrible news. Terrible.

But what the president reveals next is even more shocking to me.

"US Intelligence agencies have informed me that they have reports of sleeper cells and training schools planted in the US. These are Alliance outposts that will surely be called to action now that Canada has fallen."

Why am I suddenly sick to the pit of my stomach?

What I hear next makes me sicker still.

The teachers are applauding. Some even cheer.

At first, I'm completely confused by this. Shouldn't they be upset? We're right on the Canadian border, after all. We could be in danger.

Then I get it.

"This is a great day! Historic!" Mrs. Brewster exults. "It's happened so much sooner than we expected. We must act quickly now. Starting tonight we will begin the first phase of our plan. If US Intelligence is indeed aware of us, we can't spare a moment."

I can barely breathe. I am nauseated. Dizzy.

CMS is an Alliance training school! A sleeper cell!

Tears rise in my eyes. Evelyn has been right all along.

"I thought this day would never come!" Devi exclaims happily.

"We begin tonight!" Mrs. Brewster cries. Her voice is vibrant with triumphant joy. "We'll contact the richest and most powerful people in America and tell them that the Alliance has their spoiled brat children. If they don't do as we say, they'll never see them again. What won't parents do to protect their children? They will do anything! And they will do it for us now that we have their pampered kids. It's such a brilliant plan. Long live the Alliance!"

Chapter 16

I'm clammy cold and frozen with fear. I listen in horror as Mrs. Brewster goes on.

"Emmanuelle, here is the list of students whose parents are Alliance agents. Gather *only* those girls in the cafeteria for further instructions. Sasha, get the phones from the office so everyone else can start making calls."

I want to cry or throw up or scream, but I know that most of all, I have to move. Now! If the teachers come out and discover me, the consequences will definitely be much worse than simply being sent home.

Actually, being sent home would be a miracle right about now.

Sprinting as quietly as possible down the hall, I search for Maddie more frantically than before. Finally, finally, I find the door Evelyn told me about.

"Maddie?" I ask in a hushed tone, rapping lightly on the door. I'm down the hall and around a corner from the teachers' TV room, but they've probably split up the party by now. And who knows who else is down here, wandering the halls.

"Louisa?" Maddie answers. "I'm here, but I'm locked in from the outside."

In a stroke of crazy good luck, Rosie approaches from the opposite direction. "Maddie's in here," I tell her. "Help me find the right key to get her out."

Together we search through the keys Evelyn has given us, trying one after another. My hand shakes but I keep trying. I must stay calm. "Wait till you hear what I found out," I say to Maddie and Rosie as I try yet another key that won't work.

"What?" Rosie urges me.

I recount it all to them. When I'm done, Rosie stares at me, wide-eyed and mouth agape. "This is an Alliance training school?" she questions. "A sleeper cell? Are you sure?"

"Completely," I confirm. The key I'm testing doesn't work. Maddie's door rattles as I pull it out and try another. "Basically, we've been kidnapped. If our parents won't do as they say . . . I don't know what they plan for us. I guess they're gambling that our parents love us, and they're probably right."

"What if our parents have nothing to offer?" Rosie asks.

"If your parents have nothing to offer — not power, not influence, not money — then you wouldn't be here," I say logically.

"I suppose," Rosie says.

Unless they're already in the Alliance, I think, but I can't say it. Even in the dark hallway I can see that Rosie is pale with panic — we've had our differences, but I can't believe she knew this was coming.

"Got it!" I announce in a triumphant whisper as the key finally turns in the lock.

"I heard what you just said," Maddie informs us as

she bursts from the room. "We have to get back to the dorm to tell Evelyn."

"She has to return these keys. No one can know that we've discovered this," Rosie adds.

We race back to the dorm to find Evelyn waiting impatiently outside the door to our suite.

"What took you so long?" she cries when she sees us. "Never mind; just give me the keys!"

"Wait, wait," I say, panting from our sprint and my terror. "You have to hear this." Rosie, Maddie, and I push Evelyn into the room and start talking, quietly but fast, filling her in on everything I overheard in the main hall.

Evelyn does look a little shocked at first, but not as shocked as the rest of us. After all, she's suspected this all along. She rallies quickly. "Okay, I have maps. I re-created them from my memory on the very first day, while it was still fresh in my mind."

"We have to report this to someone," Maddie says.

"Who?" I ask.

"Someone in charge," Maddie suggests. "The police? The army?"

"But how?" Evelyn asks. "They have all our electronics — this is why they took them, so we can't communicate with anyone."

"Forget all that," Rosie says in her firm, no-nonsense team-leader voice. "We've got to get out of here. Right now."

"What about all the other girls?" Maddie asks.

"No, there's no time," Rosie says. "If everyone starts leaving, they'll know something's up. And we don't know who we can trust, do we? But we have to go. Even if CMS isn't a sleeper cell training camp —"

"Oh, it so definitely is," Evelyn interrupts her.

"Well, whatever it is, Maddie is certainly in trouble and they're bound to realize she's gone from her isolation room in the morning," Rosie says.

I'm struck with a powerful desire to go home. What good is a swimming pool if our families are at risk? It's not like Chicago is that far away from Canada, either. And if CMS — or the Alliance — has bothered to take everyone's kids . . . I just want to be with my parents, to let them know I'm safe.

"I'm leaving," I announce. "Tonight. Who else is coming with me?"

"I'm coming," Maddie says.

"All four of us should go together," Evelyn says. "We can't survive without each other." She turns to Rosie. "We're going to especially need your outdoor skills."

"I'm coming," Rosie assures us. "I don't want to be used to fight my own country. If I have to go into battle, it's going to be *against* the Alliance."

"I want to go home," I say.

"Me, too," Evelyn agrees.

"Then let's not stand here talking about it anymore," Rosie says firmly. "Evelyn, return those keys and then hurry back here. We want to be as far away as possible before they realize we're gone."

"Mrs. Brewster said they were going to contact our parents tonight," I remind them.

"Right, so we really have to move quickly," Rosie says. Evelyn heads down the hall while Maddie and I hurry into our room. "Pack up as much stuff as you can get into your backpacks," Rosie says. "It's lucky we haven't had to return our camping stuff yet. We're going to need that equipment, so pack all of that first."

Maddie and I lash our sleeping bags and ground covers back onto our backpacks. After we include all the camping stuff, we jam in as much clothing as we can fit.

Suddenly I clasp my hand over my collarbone. "My locket!" I cry, realizing it's no longer around my neck.

"Maybe it fell off in the room," Maddie suggests hopefully, and we begin looking around for it.

"What are you two looking for?" Rosie asks as we extend our search out into the living room.

"Louisa's dropped her locket somewhere," Maddie informs her.

"Why were you *wearing* it?" Rosie demands, her calm leader voice gone for the moment.

"I don't know," I moan, as I kneel by the couch to peer underneath. "I just missed them. . . ."

Rosie huffs, but she helps me and Maddie search the dorm for another fifteen minutes, until Evelyn returns. "Look what I found!" she calls happily. I jerk my head up hopefully — my locket?

But Evelyn has three packs of batteries in her arms. "I discovered the secret battery stash," she gloats. "You guys can carry those. I have more in my stash of escape-plan supplies."

Evelyn digs in the back of the only closet in the living room. She pulls out a cardboard box with a picture of carrots on its top and the NutriCorp logo. "I've been gathering stuff for this box since we got here," she reveals as she opens the top and spills out the contents.

Sugar packs, bug repellent, plastic gloves, bandages, rubber bands, paper clips, pens, and her compass are scattered on the floor. She's also managed to collect a pair of scissors, some writing stationery, and a staple remover.

"What's the staple remover for?" I ask.

"You never know what will come in handy," Evelyn replies with a shrug.

In her escape collection is a paper notebook with the map she redrew from memory on the very first day. "We can follow the highways home with this," she says. "I think it's pretty much accurate."

208

"We should stay off the main roads," Rosie disagrees. "They'll be looking for us there."

"We can follow the roads but stay in the forest," I suggest.

Rosie nods. "Yeah, we're going to have to do something like that."

Evelyn tears the map from the notebook and folds it. She slides it into the front pocket of her jeans. "Wait a minute! How could I forget this?" she cries, running into her room and returning with the map printout she showed us on our first day here. "Right now this is the most valuable thing we own," she adds as she slips it into her backpack.

Finally, we are packed and ready to leave.

The four of us gather by the front door. "Have we forgotten anything?" Rosie asks as she scans the room we've called home for more than two weeks.

Maddie crosses to the oil lamp and lifts it, picking up the matches that we kept there. "These will come in handy," she says, pocketing them.

"It sure beats rubbing two sticks together for a spark," Evelyn agrees.

Rosie crosses to the table to grab her copy of *Julie of the Wolves*. "I never did finish it, and it could make good reading around a campfire."

The image of us all sleeping out in the open around a fire night after night frightens me. And it's September — it's going to get colder, and soon.

"Can I have another five minutes to look for my locket?" I request.

"There's no time," Rosie says. "Sorry, Louisa."

I know she's right.

There's no choice. We can't stay here.

The four of us leave the room. Moving quietly and quickly, we go down the fire stairs at the end of the hallway. Maddie pushes open the door and we stand in the brilliant illumination of the full moon's second night.

"We need to get under the trees," Rosie says. "In this light, anyone looking out a window will see us."

One by one, each of us makes a dash for the darkness of the surrounding forest. When we're all together again, Evelyn consults her compass. "That way is south," she says, pointing into the trees. "South is what we want."

The four of us begin walking, leaving CMS behind.

And none of us knows what lies ahead.

What will happen tomorrow?
Read on for a preview of
Tomorrow Girls #2: Run for Cover.

"Shhhh," Evelyn says. "They might have bugged the trees." Her dark skin blends into the shadows, but in the glimmers of moonlight, I can see her eyes darting around in that annoying, *everybody's after us* way she has that drives me crazy.

"Bugged the *trees*?" Louisa says. "That's a little paranoid, even for you."

Evelyn flares up at once. "I might be paranoid, but I'm right, aren't I? I mean, I was right about the school!"

I roll my eyes. "Maybe one or two of your insane theories were right, but when you're shooting a million ideas into the sky, it's not surprising that a couple of them will land."

"I was right that it was a conspiracy!" Evelyn's voice is getting too loud. "The Alliance *was* luring us into a trap! The secret locations, the weird classes, taking away all our electronics — it was all part of their plan!"

"Shh, all right," Louisa says. "We're not disagreeing with you. You were right all along. You're a conspiracy-detecting genius. Is that what you want to hear?"

"Can we keep moving, please?" I say. Maddie sighs loudly, but she doesn't argue as we start walking again. I would rather try to find our way in the dark, letting our eyes adjust, but not enough moonlight penetrates the thick canopy of branches, so we have to use a flashlight.

I let Louisa hold it, since she has a steady hand. Twigs and pine needles crackle and snap under our feet, and we're surrounded by the Christmas smell of the pine forest. If our situation weren't so utterly terrifying, it would be kind of nice and peaceful out here.

"I don't understand their plan, though, Evelyn," Maddie says after a minute. "If they were planning to hold us hostage for our parents' money, why would they teach us survival skills and all that other stuff? Why train us like we're soldiers? We'd never fight for the Alliance, no matter what they did to brainwash us!"

"Too right," I say. "I'd break Mrs. Brewster's face before I ever helped the Alliance."

"Wow, Rosie," Louisa says. "Tell us how you really feel. No, I'm kidding. I agree with you." A low-hanging branch snags her blond hair and she stops to disentangle herself.

"Maybe —" Evelyn says, and then pauses. Her shoulders are hunched and her hands are shoved in her jeans pockets.

"Maybe what?" I say.

"Never mind," she mumbles. "You'll just think it's stupid."

"I won't," Maddie says, bumping her shoulder. "Go ahead and tell us. I like hearing your theories."

I exchange a glance with Louisa. In the dark I can't see her expression, but I'm sure she's thinking what I am — that it's kind of annoying how Evelyn and Maddie always stick together and encourage each other's worst impulses. I don't say anything, though. As long as we're still walking, leaving CMS behind us, I don't care how much talking everyone else needs to do at the same time. If I were them, I'd be saving my energy, but I can only boss them around so much without someone snapping. I need to pick my battles.

"Well," Evelyn says, "I was just thinking . . . maybe not all the girls there were hostages. Maybe some of them were really on the Alliance's side." She hurries on before we can respond. "I mean, we don't really know anything about them. Maybe a lot of the others were being trained to fight in the War, and they knew it was secretly an Alliance training camp the whole time."

"I did hear something like that," Louisa says slowly. "The teachers were talking about getting certain girls to the cafeteria for a debriefing or something. The kids of Alliance parents."

We all fall silent. I think about my friends at CMS — Mary Jensen and Chui-lian Lee especially. I miss them. They would be a lot more useful out here than Evelyn and Maddie — that's for sure. I'd also take Anne or Erica or Rae or Carole over them any day. But were they all lying to me? Were they secretly working for the Alliance? Would they have turned on me and helped to hold me hostage if — when — everything came out in the open?

"I don't believe it," I say, but my voice catches, and I don't sound as confident as I want to.

Of course, part of me can't help wondering . . . if it's true, is the secret I'm keeping any better than theirs?

POISON APPLE BOOKS

The Dead End

This Totally Bites!

Miss Fortune

Now You See Me...

Midnight Howl

Her Evil Twin

THRILLING. BONE-CHILLING. THESE BOOKS HAVE BITE!